RENAISSANCE

Beauty

A NOVEL

RENAISSANCE *Beauty*

A NOVEL

HEATHER SIMONSEN

spring creek
BOOK COMPANY
Provo, Utah

ISBN 13: 978-1-932898-35-4
ISBN 10:1-932898-35-2
e. 1

Published by:
Spring Creek Book Company
P.O. Box 50355
Provo, Utah 84605-0355

www.springcreekbooks.com

Cover design © Spring Creek Book Company
Cover design by Nicole Cunningham
Back cover artwork: Lucrezia Panciatichi portrait painted by Agnolo Bronzino, approximately 1540 A.D. Galleria degli Uffizi, Florence, Italy.

Printed in the United States of America
10 9 8 7 6 5 4 3 2 1
Printed on acid-free paper

Library of Congress Cataloging-in-Publication Data

Simonsen, Heather, 1970-
  Renaissance beauty / by Heather Simonsen.
     p. cm.
  ISBN-13: 978-1-932898-35-4 (pbk. : alk. paper)
  ISBN-10: 1-932898-35-2 (pbk. : alk. paper)
  1. Mormons--Juvenile fiction. 2. Christian life--Juvenile fiction. I. Title.
  PZ7.S6057947Ren 2005

                    2005006809

Dedication

For Soren

Acknowledgments

I express my deepest gratitude to Mollie Davenport for being my close friend and first editor of this novel. Thanks for believing in me. Next, I appreciate my editor Rachelle Christensen for her excellent work, talent and thoroughness. To my publishers, Chad and Tammy Daybell, thanks for being a dream to work with. To my friends, you make my life so sweet. To my darling family, you are my inspiration. To the love of my life, Soren: thanks for giving me halcyon years and a deep reservoir of everlasting joy. Halle and Christian, I love you to infinity and b-e-y-o-n-d.

"You are the hero of your own story."

—Eleanor Roosevelt

1

I peeled off my favorite sweater, chucked it on the monster couch and headed to the kitchen for some graham crackers to dip in a glass of milk. It was my ritual, dousing the cracker just long enough so that when I lifted it to my mouth it melted on my tongue, but not so long that it fell into my cup in a soggy mess. It was a delicate balance.

I had been at Barclay's all day and headed home as the sun was going down, as Mom required. Barclay's kitchen was never stocked with fresh milk and the cupboards were almost always bare. His sullen mother couldn't drag herself to the grocery store. Barclay survived on the frozen pizzas his dad left for him stacked high in the freezer. The scarcity of my favorite snack at Barclay's house only made my craving stronger.

It was late fall and the air was brisk and chilly. There was a slight fresh scent of pine mixed in, too. Before I made it to the kitchen, I noticed something that gave me an uneasy feeling. Like when you are standing on an unstable bridge and your legs are mush, and with just the slightest wrong movement you could fall to your untimely death. I suppose the signs had been there for a while. Mom and Dad had been fighting a lot, but as a kid, you just never imagine that it could actually happen.

There on the mud colored floor in the kitchen were two leather suitcases and a duffle bag in a neat row. My first thought, in an effort to calm myself down, was that we were going to take a weekend trip I'd forgotten about. How wrong I was. When I saw Dad's face, I knew something was terribly wrong. He appeared to be in agony, with dark circles under his eyes, though he was trying to smile. My mom was behind him, crying, her eyes were puffy, with her arms folded and resting on her waist. She, too, forced a grin.

"I have to leave, Avie, sweetheart. I'm so sorry, but Daddy has to go away for a while." He knelt down beside me and I instinctively wrapped my arms around his neck and breathed in the familiar smell of Old Spice. His cheek was just slightly stubbly, his shoulders strong and broad.

"What do you mean, Dad?" I had a terrible lump in my throat and a sense of panic. I thought I might collapse. My white, chubby legs started to tremble.

"I mean that Mommy and Daddy can't live together anymore. But, honey, you listen to me." He held my pale face in his large hands. "That will never, never change how I feel about you. I love you, sweet pea, you mean everything to me."

I couldn't control the choking sobs that wracked my body.

"But where are you going, Daddy?"

"I'm going to live at a different house, sweetie, one you'll really like! You can come see me as soon as tomorrow! Won't that be fun?" He was desperately trying to wipe my tears. "It has a swimming pool."

I turned to my mother with anger. "Mom? Is this true? How can Daddy be leaving? Tell him to stay!" I ran over to her and before I even realized what I was doing I started hitting her with my fists. She was now crying louder, our sobs mixing together in a sad cacophony.

Dad pulled me away and whispered words in my ear I don't even remember. Everything was a blur, a jumble of disillusionment and betrayal. It felt surreal. I didn't know what it felt like to faint.

But I was light-headed, cold and sweaty all at the same time. All this emotion was compounded by a sense of guilt I had from the image that popped into my mind of my dad and me floating on our backs together in a beautiful, blue pool. I squinted to force the image away. I was conflicted, ashamed and felt the first real pangs I can remember of being lonely. I'll never forget how that felt.

When Dad finally picked up his suitcases, walked to the front door and opened it, I dove for his leg. I held on to his ankle for all I was worth, noticing the navy socks he was wearing, the same socks he took out of his neat bottom drawer each morning.

"Don't go, Dad! You can't leave! Daddy, Daddy, no! Daddy, take me with you. Dad!" I was hysterical.

While my dad gently peeled me off of him, my mom came and wrapped her arms around me from behind.

"It's going to be all right, honey," she kept saying into my ear in a flat, even voice. "We are going to be just fine, sugar plum, just fine." But in her embrace, I felt fear.

⊹⊱✦⊰⊹

I learned later that Daddy had fallen in love with his secretary, Janet. She was about ten years younger than Mom and Dad, and I remember her being very pretty. Dad would come and get me on weekends and take me to the zoo or to dinner a lot that first year after they split. But once he and Janet had a baby boy, named Cole, it was really all over for me. Dad stopped calling, and even when I called him he was preoccupied and seemingly uninterested. They had a baby girl, Casey, two years after that. It was as if Dad had exchanged Mom and me for a brand new family, with a prettier Mommy and it was more than heart breaking.

He invited me over for Christmas and Thanksgiving, big holidays like that, but I hated his little kids. I was so jealous of them. I couldn't stand to even be near them. And Janet would always come over all sugary sweet and try to talk to me, hand me a gift she'd picked out and wrapped in a big red bow. Every time I stared at her, with her freshly styled and highlighted hair, makeup just so, I loathed her more. She was the reason my family fell apart. So Dad invited me over less and less and this was just fine by me.

Years passed and I found that I needed him the most when I was in high school. I felt so vulnerable and left out all the time. But Daddy was into his new family and was pretty much nonexistent in my life. I'm sure Janet sensed my disdain for her and the kids. Once, I ripped a toy horse out of Cole's little fingers and he started bawling. I wasn't sure if Dad or Janet saw me from the other room. I hid Casey's favorite little ducky in a linen closet upstairs and shrugged my shoulders innocently when Dad asked if I'd seen it. I was old enough to know better. When I returned home, I couldn't believe I was bullying my half brother and sister. After all, they were just little kids. In a way, I had tested Dad to see if he'd choose them over me again. He did. I'd never felt so lonely.

I'd sit in church and listen to my Young Women's leaders talk about the importance of family. They'd talk about how "families could be together forever" and I always wanted to cry. I'd try to hide these feelings. I knew a leader would pull me aside and try to talk to me about the divorce. Though well intentioned, this never made me feel better. Nothing would. The facts were the facts. I remember one leader looking at me nervously for any sign of discomfort, trying desperately to tailor her thoughts to fit my circumstances. "Things that don't work out in this life will be worked out in Heaven. The Lord's time is different than our own."

This too gave me little solace. I wanted my dad now. I missed him. I wanted to feel safe again, complete, like a real family. Mom didn't even cook anymore. I was lucky if I got macaroni and cheese out of a box. I knew Janet loved to cook and this knowledge only angered me more. And Mom was always teary. She would fall apart if she couldn't open up a jar of peanut butter. We were in bad shape.

I buried my nose in my dog Tigger's fur when I got home from school each day. It helped to feel her softness against my face. Tigger was always there for me, her eyes holding such understanding and even offering a little wink now and then.

Barclay came over all the time. As the years passed with no father in the house, he helped with little utilitarian tasks like unclogging sinks or fixing a screen door, things my mom had never learned how to do. It was a comfort having him around, though my mom never appreciated him, despite being desperate for help.

I felt Barclay enjoyed spending time with us. His mom was becoming more and more dark and elusive by the day. Despite his own difficult circumstances, things seemed to brighten up when Barclay walked through the door. His slouchy walk and mischievous grin always made me feel calm. I loved the way his longish, brown hair would cover his left eye and he would shake it back in one swift jerking motion. Barclay was predictable and kind. He lent some normalcy in our lives at a time when both Mom and I were spinning out of control.

❧❧❧

I found comfort in books, which became my friends. I would stay up late using a flashlight under the covers to read. They were salves at times when I missed Dad so much. That's when I developed a unique ability to bond with an inanimate object. I'd carry the books around with me during the day, long after I'd read and re-read them many times. Even if I knew full well I wouldn't have a chance to read a single page, I'd tote them along just to touch the cover, flip through the pages and breathe in their musty scent. At first it was *Pippy Longstocking, Where the Red Fern Grows* and *My Friend Flicka* that became my companions. I had a mad, secret crush on Ken and imagined one day we'd ride Flicka together. Once, I insisted on bringing all three books with us to Wal-Mart to get some new shoes. My mom thought it was strange and enforced a new rule that I keep all the books at home on the messy, crowded shelves. I circumvented this edict by stuffing my "book friends" surreptitiously in my backpack or in an over-sized purse.

Later, it was *Jane Eyre, Little Women,* and *To Kill a Mockingbird* which would keep me company at night and give me a break from my mother. It was a way to step in someone else's shoes for a moment and drift away. I'd find myself at difficult moments asking, "What would Scout do?"

My senior year had been emotionally excruciating. A time that, I guess, should've been idyllic, was plain awful. I seemed to stumble over my clumsy feet, trying desperately to fit in. I did a good job of making a fool of myself. Good thing I had *Huckleberry Finn* to lean on. Still, even the works of Mark Twain couldn't save me from myself.

A week before prom, I saw Tommy Anderson working at the front desk at the library. He was the cutest guy in the senior class, lots of wavy blond hair and ice blue eyes. I had been sitting there alone again, in the library, and my mind drifted off into a moment of insanity. I sauntered up to where Tommy sat, never having talked to him in my life, leaned up against the librarian's counter, oh so nonchalantly, and opened my big mouth. Out came these words:

"You know the big dance is this weekend . . ." pause, pause, eternally long pause. He looked at me with a dumbfounded expression as if to say, "And your point is?" What an idiot I was.

I turned and ran out of the library, down the crowded halls of West High, and fumbled with my locker combination. When I finally got it opened, I ducked my head in and cried, hoping no one would see me. That's one of those days you wish you were an adult who could just choose to leave early. I, of course, was stuck there to suffer through the last period, Mr. Kettle's chemistry class, touching my book like a child fondles a favorite blanket.

When I got home from school, I decided not to let my mom in on my discouragement. If I'd told her what I'd done, she would've said the same things the voice that told me I was an idiot had. So, I remained vague, telling her I was tired but everything was fine, just fine. I needed a few days of strength to tell her that I had no date to the prom. After a dinner of macaroni and cheese made from a box one night, I finally explained that I wouldn't be going. She pursed her lips together and said, "That's okay, not a big deal." But her lips quivered and her eyes conveyed discouragement. It was clear that I had let her down. I headed straight to my room to talk to Atticus Finch.

❧❦❧

I somehow made it through those tumultuous years of high school, but after graduation, one trip would change everything.

Grams, Papa and I had just arrived in Italy. I felt groggy and exhausted from falling asleep upright in my seat on the airplane but not really resting properly, and waking feeling sore and more tired than before when we finally landed.

Grams was dressed to the nines for traveling, like always. In her day, air travel made you a part of an elite group. She wore a cream colored hat with a bouquet of pink and purple flowers, and yellow daisies around the brim. She had a butter yellow silk scarf draped around her neck and a long, beaded necklace the color of irises with matching dangle earrings. Her cream linen tunic nearly reached her knees. Underneath that, she wore pink spandex stretch pants. And her shoes were gold, low-heeled sandals dotted with yellow silk flowers similar to the ones on her hat.

After landing in Rome, we walked through the jet way and the humid heat of Italy hit us like a sauna. I noticed that the colorful flowers on Grams' hat had not faired well on the flight. They were all smashed from when the flight attendant had to fold it up and put it in the overhead compartment. It was too large to fit underneath the chair in front of Grams. She'd thrown a fit but, thankfully, Papa intervened, imparting a little sanity to the situation. Papa always was the calm one.

With slow, languid movements, trying to stretch my stiff limbs, I followed Grams and Papa down the stairs to the baggage claim.

With each step downward I was walking into a different world. The people were a sea of tawny skin the color of caramel and onyx black hair. The rest were obviously tourists from all over the world, with their cameras around their necks, maps in their satchels, and wrinkled clothing after the long flight. They wore expressions of wonder.

It was the beginning of my transformation.

From Rome, we boarded an ancient-looking bus that appeared to be older than the Sistine Chapel. The clunker jostled us like passengers on a roller coaster on the rickety streets during the long journey to Florence. I was worried for Grams and Papa but they held on tight to their seats and adjusted well.

We rested at our hotel. The room was much smaller and cramped than I had imagined. I later learned that small quarters are typical in Italy. Our room was so tiny that Grams, Papa and I had to stack our suitcases on top of one another in the corner of the room in order to navigate from the tall beds to the bathroom. The beds felt amazing though, full of cushiony down, like folding up in yards of soft quilt batting to go to sleep.

A nice, long shower brought me back to life. Evening was falling on Florence as we walked out of the hotel and into the city center. The narrow streets were crowded and full of vendors with their little rolling carts filling the air with chatter. The sweet aroma of bread baking in the ovens wafted through the air as we stepped up on the sidewalk and passed a *café* called *"Trattoria da Zá Zá."* I tipped my head back and looked up at the striking building. Written in bold black letters on the awnings that were the color of navel oranges were the words: *Matrimoni, Cena, y Riuoni.* There must have been many important moments celebrated inside those glass doors, I thought. I peeked through the windows. How many jubilant Italian brides danced underneath those chandeliers?

The air in this ancient city was electric. I felt more alive and full of wonder than ever before. I was aware of every detail of my new surroundings; small things caught my eye as if I were watching the nuances of an opera unfolding on stage.

A *Vespa* swooshed past us. Grams, with all of her moxie, shouted mild curses at the empty air after him. "That'll teach him to mess with these Americans," she said. I shook my head.

"*Scusi,* you lika de *Firenze*?" A deep, raspy voice boomed. He was a thin Italian man with flecks of gray in his longish hair. He had heavy bags underneath his deep brown eyes from a life full of adventure. A wide smile stretched across his gold-capped teeth. I'm sure many a lady swooned when she saw those dimples. "De city? You lika de city?" He asked, gesturing with a paint-splattered brush in his hands. I noticed he was cradling a small, white canvas.

"Yes—yes, very much, THANK YOU." I spoke much slower and louder than necessary, as if shouting my words would help him understand my English. "What are you painting?"

"Ah, I don't knows justa yet. The image, whatever I want to paint has to, how you say? Catch my eye, taka my breath from my chest." He put his thick hand, dirty with dried paint, firmly over his broad chest. His shirt was unbuttoned, revealing black, curly chest hair. "*Comprendere? Si?* You understand what I say?"

Over my shoulder, Grams was elbow deep in leather bags at one of the little stands. Papa patiently stood behind scanning the Florence skyline for landmarks. That would keep them busy for at least a little while.

"I do understand, I think," I responded to the painter. "You're saying that your subject has to be beautiful in order for you to paint it." I stepped closer to the Italian man. "You know, they say, beauty's in the eye of the beholder. Do you think there's any truth to that?"

The painter squinted at me as if he were at sea trying to find dry land.

A friend from our ward who had served a mission in Italy had told me that Italians won't admit it if they don't know something, or don't understand. It's considered rude. While Americans might say easily in conversation, "I don't know, what do you think?" Italians will just keep talking offering you the many morsels of knowledge that they do know, however impertinent. I kept this in mind as we spoke.

"Ah, *si*." He gestured with both hands as if he were wiping a canvas clean. "You see, there's so mucha more to beauty than just good looks. How you say in English, character? Yes, dats it. 'Di character' makes a great beauty, and a painting. She cannot be, ah, just attractive. Must have some, strength and goodness behind all dat. Tink about de *Mona Lisa*. She was not lika princessa, not a great beauty, *non*."

"Too bad that's not how the world works," I said. Why was I telling him all this? Why did I trust this stranger so implicitly? "It can be a pretty cruel place. I just graduated from high school. I'm so glad to be finished with that. I want to learn how to hold my head high, find my own way in the world. Problem is, I don't have a clue how to do that."

I noticed he was working furiously now with his brush. What was he doing? His eyes darted from the canvas back to me in rapid movements. It made me nervous, so I filled the silence with words.

"I've always struggled to try and fit in, be prettier, thinner, more attractive to boys. I don't know, maybe I'm worrying about the wrong things. Maybe, I should just give up." I had no idea why I was confiding such deep feelings to a complete stranger, in a foreign country, no less. Maybe it was something about his infectious smile or the way he worked the brush on canvas with the tenderness and confidence of a mother coaxing her children.

"What es your name?" He asked.

"Avery Rose. We're here visiting from Salt Lake City, Utah. I'll be starting at the University of Utah in the fall. This is my last shindig before I have to get serious about stuff, I guess." It was a habit of mine to rattle on filling silence when I was nervous. I offered him my hand but saw he was still furiously working on his masterpiece.

I was breaking all the rules my mother had taught me about not talking to strangers. Something about this painter made me want to open up to him and tell him all about me. Was it the smile lines around his eyes that formed into deep crevices from too much painting in the sun? Or could it have been my strange, new surroundings and the residual jet lag that marred my judgment? What was the harm of talking to this stranger, anyway? Was he going to track me down a million miles away back in Utah? Somehow, though exhilarated, I felt safe.

"Nice to meet you Avery Rose, *di* Salt Lake City, Utah. I'm Giuseppe Luchetti."

"It's nice to meet you, too, Giuseppe. So, are you going to be one of 'the greats' one day? Will I see your work in the famous galleries eventually? I mean, that's why you are doing this, right? To be the very best, a famous painter, a future *Da Vinci*?"

"Ah, no." He crinkled his brow again, making the deep lines in his face even deeper. His skin was the color of hot chocolate with a little melted marshmallow mixed in. "I paint because I love to paint. Dat is all. It is my job in life. To paint, and paint de best dat I can. I like de first stroke on an empty canvas as much as de moment I finish de last detail. Dats how you know it is your dream, and not the dream of another. You are happiest doing it, when you enjoy de journey, you are fulfilling your destination."

"You mean 'your destiny?'"

"Ah, yes, destiny. Of course!"

He slapped his thigh and let out a belly laugh. Then he went back to working furiously on his mysterious piece. Giuseppe oozed deep feelings and wisdom underneath his tough wrinkles.

He didn't take his eyes off of me while he was painting. A young woman walked by. Her hair was black like a raven and fell to her hip in one smooth sheath. She was so lovely that she could've been on a fashion catwalk here or anywhere.

"I'll never be beautiful like her. I have to face facts."

"*Scusi*, Avery, don't be so sure. Don't be so sure."

"Why, an Italian painter, Avery! How very quaint and so Italian," Grams' strident voice pierced my ears. I felt her grip on my arm.

"Well, we are in Italy," Papa mused with sarcasm on his tongue. "You really are so observant, Diane, I'll give you that."

"Oh shush, now!" Grams elbowed Papa gently and smiled big at Giuseppe Luchetti. Hot pink lipstick was smudged on her too-white teeth. I tapped my tooth to let her know, but she was too engrossed in conversation. "This nice gentleman probably needs peace and quiet for the masterpiece he's working on."

Grams tapped her foot, waiting for a reply. Finally she continued: "What are you working on there?"

"Ah, it 'tis a surprise. But I'll tell you dis: it will be *una* magnificent work of art."

"Could we take a picture of you, sir? With our granddaughter, Avery? This is such a special trip for her." Grams pinched my cheek, like I was five years old again. "It would be such a neat memento for her."

"*Una fotografia? Buono.* Okay, no problem."

I smiled as Grams captured this moment in time, the painter Giuseppe on the edge of Florence and me, his secret canvas, and the city behind us. What was he painting?

✳✳✳

I returned again and again to this same spot on my daily journeys to the town square. Each time I'd stop and talk with the painter for a few moments. And each time, when I left to explore this hot, magical city, Giuseppe would thank me saying, "*Grazie, grazie.* You come see me again, *pronto, sì?*" He would flash me a wide, gold-filled smile, showing those pronounced caverns in his face, as if he'd been waiting for me to walk down the uneven cobblestone streets for a long time.

2

In those eyes, those lovely oval windows, there were endless possibilities. Framed by the ethereal, thin eyebrows, no doubt those who gazed into this 16th century woman's hazel eyes dreamed of loving her forever. Standing there in front of the painting *Lucrezia Panciatichi's* skin looked luminous, like milk, her scarlet hair parted in the middle, braided at the nape of her neck, and wrapped around her head in a neat mound. The Florentine lady looking back at me from the canvas of oils must have been revered as angelic and comely in her time. Certainly that was why the High Renaissance artist *Bronzino* chose her as his subject. Her high forehead and her long, prominent nose and tiny demure mouth with barely a chin at all were the characteristics of the gifted, those bestowed with the exquisite beauty of the era.

I was 18 years old. I'd be starting college at the University of Utah in the fall on scholarship. I had excelled academically at West High, an achievement that had given me many colleges to choose from. Inside, I always felt scarred, broken down and incomplete, even here in the glorious city of Florence. I was glad that *Catcher in the Rye* was keeping me company in my backpack during the trip. I had a serious crush on Holden. I was sure that I could understand him like no one else. I thought I alone could change him.

But there, in the *Uffizi* Gallery, all my grand plans for the future seemed so far away. Little did I know that a painting there would change the course of my life.

"Like looking in a mirror, isn't it Avery," Grams said. Her words catapulted me back into the present and made me feel empty, like most of her comments. She had always judged me nearly as harshly as my mother. But with Grams, her ability to filter her remarks had waned with age. The filter that at one time told her what not to say had disappeared altogether. Her comments always began innocuously enough, but a verbal punch in the gut was usually the end result. Listening to her talk was like watching a pot of hot water begin to boil. At first, the water under flame appears calm, then a few bubbles rise, and finally turns into a rolling boil.

"If you had lived back then, why, they would've had to chase the boys away with a stick!" Grams said, her manicured nails resting on her white leather arm purse, hot pink lips lined outside her actual lip line to appear larger. She wore a shiny gold lamé tunic, large gold earrings and matching brooch, and white pants. "You wouldn't have had to sit all alone the night of the prom, no ma'am," she sighed and looked up at the museum's grand ceiling. "All of your friends with their pretty corsages on their wrists while you were drowning your sorrows in Häagen-Dazs. Now that was the last thing you needed, extra weight on your thighs." She clucked pity with her tongue.

"Grams, please!" I stepped forward, trying to get out of her line of fire, putting a safe few feet between us. "I'd just as soon forget about that night, thank you very much. Why do you have to continually bring it up?" I didn't stick around for her reply. I turned and walked away.

I was mesmerized by the images before me. And it was true, what Grams had said. I did look like the women in these masterpieces. This realization fascinated me but sent me reeling into a dank, depressed mood. What was the use of wondering what life would've been like for me back then, if I lived in a time when I fit in?

I moved through the cold, silent gallery looking at works by *Beccafumi* and *Cellini*. The women in the portraits truly were exquisite, though they looked nothing like the movie stars I saw on the big screen at the Cinemark near our dull white house in Salt Lake City. My leather sandals on the polished stone floors softly marked my passage through the High Renaissance section of the museum.

As I looked at the paintings, I thought about what was considered beautiful, how blonde and tan, with a voluptuous yet trim figure was the ideal. Jennifer Aniston hair with a Jennifer Lopez body was what everyone was trying for, even going under the knife to achieve. Plastic surgeons were racking up trips to Brazil to posh resorts thanks to many girls' wishes to feel loved. In fact, Sally Johnston, one of the popular girls at my school, was probably at the hospital in recovery as I walked through the gallery. Her mother had given her a breast augmentation for graduation. What happened to the monogrammed duffle bag as the traditional gift? Believe it or not, I knew others who begged their parents for eyebrow lifts and got them.

I noticed a museum docent staring at me and forcing a taut smile across her face. She spoke in a thick Italian accent, her black bifocals resting on her slim nose as she worked on the stack of papers in her lap.

"Ah, you are a fan of *Boticelli?* He is my favorite," she said, motioning with her eyes toward the painting in front of me. Her hair was in a slick, low bun. I had been staring at it for some time, but my mind had been elsewhere.

"Oh, this, ah yes. It's quite a masterpiece," I said, fumbling for the right words.

"You are American, *no?*" she asked, adjusting her glasses so she could see me through the top half of her lenses.

"Yes. We're from Utah. Those are my grandparents," I pointed to Grams and Papa, admiring a painting in the distance. "I just graduated from high school. This is my big trip, you know, I guess the one where I find myself."

"Hmmmm," the docent furrowed her brow. "To find yourself? Quite da journey, *si?*" The docent studied me like a complex work of art. "Must know who you are, before you share life with another? Da greatest quest, *no?* To find *amore*. Love. He never did," she said focusing her eyes once again on the painting.

"Who?" I asked, unsure of where this conversation was going.

"Boticelli," she answered, with an exasperated look that said she believed the answer was obvious. "Very lonely man all his life," she said, shaking her head and clucking her tongue. "What talent, though, *no?* De talent, de gifts. Madness fueled his passion for de painting. Too bad, *no?* A great artist, *si*, but a life with *amore? No.*"

As suddenly as the woman became interested in me, she buried herself again in her paperwork, sending me the unmistakable message our discussion was over.

I headed for the door marked *Il Bagno;* a few too many Diet Cokes made my bladder feel like it was about to burst. Plus, I desperately needed to take a break and collect myself before heading off to heaven knows where with Grams and Papa, probably traipsing through every landmark in the vicinity, no matter how unimportant. Don't get me wrong. I love my grandparents. I just have to pace myself a little with them. You know, just spread out the joy of their company a little and try to maintain my sanity along the way.

My grandparents brought me here to Florence as a rite of passage, I suppose.

Grams and Papa insisted I come to the Uffizi Gallery to see some of the Italian Renaissance paintings since the moment we arrived in Italy. I dreaded it, feigning interest in other tourist attractions to avoid the topic altogether. My whole life they had told me how I would've fit in better in that time.

"A true Renaissance beauty," Grams would say, thinking she was giving me real comfort. But of course, I wanted to hear how gorgeous I was today, last time I checked time travel was still impossible. *Michelangelo's* prodigies weren't really possible suitors for me.

Grams and Papa took each one of their grandchildren abroad when they graduated from high school. I guess it was my turn to become cultured. With my history as their little "Renaissance beauty," Italy was an easy choice for a destination. Of course they never consulted me.

Though I didn't know it then, the issues I had to work out were much more than skin deep. I never dreamed a woman, depicted in a painting, who had lived centuries before me would be the impetus for my spiritual transformation. I was about to learn what it means to be a true friend to someone in need. In the process, I'd learn how to love myself, and along the way, I'd balance on that elusive tight rope of falling in love.

As we headed toward the exit I touched my own thin, wispy, uncooperative red hair and put a finger to my small, thin lips. I've always hated how no amount of time spent in the sun slathered with oil would yield a tan. My skin is nearly as white as an albino, and that's no exaggeration. It's virtually impossible for me to find the right color of make-up foundation.

As Grams berated Papa about something, and it was always something, I stole away, back to the *Bronzino*. I had to get a glimpse of *Lucrezia*, the beauty in oil, one more time.

As I stood there concentrating on the magnificent detail of her, the pendant necklace around her long neck, the dark background that made her gentle features even more magical, I imprinted her into my mind. Then I went to the gallery's gift shop and asked for a post card of the painting. I wanted to take her back with me to Salt Lake so I could take her out, hold her in the palm of my hand, and gaze at her in those moments when I felt like I had a large "L" attached to my forehead for "Loser." Maybe she could give me the confidence I needed, a way to feel proud of the way I looked. There was no doubt in my mind I'd need to summon her image soon. So, I delicately tucked the post card in a small pocket in my purse where *Lucrezia* could stay among my lipstick, compact, and wallet to comfort me.

The tempting smell of garlic, tomatoes, and olive oil wafted through the air as I walked the main thoroughfare with Grams and Papa. Small cars, miniature by American standards, sped over the cobblestone streets. As we passed along on the sidewalks, laden with tourists and people on bicycles, I peered over my shoulder to my left down the small side streets. In between the ancient rock buildings of the main thoroughfare were alleyways filled with shops, apartments, hostels and restaurants only maneuverable on foot, bike or by the small *Vespa* scooters. Very tiny cars narrowly squeaked by. These alleyways were small arteries bringing life to the heart of the city. They were filled with the voices of laughing children and the echo of chatter, punctuated by the occasional loud argument between shop owners or even a lovers' spat. A young couple sat close together on iron chairs at a café at the entrance of one of the narrow side streets dining on pasta and tomatoes, mindlessly dipping their crusted Italian bread in white ceramic plates of oil, never taking their eyes off one another. I longed to feel that way about someone.

East of Eden accompanied me in my backpack along with *Wuthering Heights.* Every now and then, I'd get them out, touch their weathered spines, and then reach down and touch the post card of the painting tucked inside my purse. I found myself wondering if *Lucrezia* had ever walked this very same path.

While continuing on the main road that leads to the heart of Florence, we entered an area of bustling culture and commerce. A rotund middle-aged Italian man wearing an apron shouted to us about the high quality of his leather:

"*Favore,* look at this! De best in *Firenze, no?*" He shouted.

There were racks of bright-colored dresses and sashes next to him, warm hues of ochre, peach and scarlet. A woman with her black curls piled high on her head in a messy bun stood nearby.

Papa motioned for us to stop at one of the *gelaterias* to get the treat that had become our staple while in Italy.

An Italian boy my age looked at us with enormous brown eyes. Then, he spoke to us from across the counter. "You like some, *si*? Coconut with rice, mango, blue berries, hazelnuts, raspberries, walnuts or pecans. Delicious, *no*?

"Yes, please. I'll have the coconut with rice, mango and hazelnuts. Thank you, I mean, *grazie.*"

"Ah, why don't you make that three, dear boy," said Grams, and she flashed him a flirtatious smile with her too-white fake teeth. Grams wore a mint green pantsuit and a silk scarf that didn't quite match her clunky sandals.

We sat at a small metal table that had white tile insets. I savored the cool, flavorful treat, letting it roll around in my mouth and melt on my tongue.

Papa was stirring his *gelato* idly and Grams was picking out the coconut with her long, red fingernails.

"I don't know why I didn't tell him I hate coconut. Why, it just sounded so appealing when he said it," Grams said.

"You probably wouldn't even notice it, Diane, if you'd just let it be. It all mixes together nicely. You always have to pick, pick, pick over everything," retorted Papa.

"Well excuse me," Grams snapped. "Sorry I don't eat my

gelato like you expect me to, George. I didn't know there were rules surrounding it. Sheesh." Grams rolled her eyes and gave me a look as if we were both in cahoots against Papa.

"So Avery," she added another chunk of coconut to the pile resting on her napkin, "What's your plan, dear?"

I didn't know what to say. She raised her eyebrows and her shoulders with one hand outstretched, waiting for my answer.

"You know, your future! What are you going to do with your life? What will your major be? What about your career? Marriage? You should really be thinking about these things."

A man on a bicycle whizzed past, jingling his bell at tourists to get out of the way or be flattened. I was grateful for the diversion.

"Diane, she's only 18. You certainly didn't have it all figured out at that age," offered Papa.

"You can say that again. That's when I married you!" Grams laughed at her own joke. Papa wasn't smiling.

"Back to your questions," I interrupted, desperate to restore the peace. "For one thing, I'm not even dating anyone, Grams, so marriage is out of the question. But as for the near future, maybe I'll major in art history. I've enjoyed the paintings at the *Uffizi* Gallery so much, I guess, well, they've inspired me."

"Oh good heaven's, child," Grams wrinkled her brow. "What would you actually do with a degree like that? It's useless. Learn a trade, and then visit the galleries. Why, I don't see how you could possibly make a life out of studying art. Really, Avery."

"Why not? Why not immerse myself in it? Maybe I would do quite well."

Grams waved her hand in the air dismissively. "I'm sure you would, dear. I'm just saying, why, you've got your whole life ahead of you. You don't want to make any big mistakes now." Her voice became a whisper. "Wouldn't want to go down the wrong path, now would we?"

"Let the poor girl be, Diane. She needs to find her own way." Papa patted me on the back and then slurped down the rest of his *gelato*, tipping his head back.

"Well, I'm just saying it's good to have a skill. You know, something useful. Especially since, as you admitted, you probably won't be getting married anytime soon. You've got to be able to take care of yourself one day." Grams' voice was strident and annoying. She made my love life sound so hopeless. Who was she to say marriage was nowhere in my future? Maybe I didn't even want it, now or ever. Would that be so bad? I tried to console myself with these questions.

"Course," Grams pushed her empty cup away from her and crumpled up the napkin with the coconut. "There's always a mission. If you're not getting married anytime soon, you could always serve a mission."

I knew this was coming.

Sitting there at the *gelateria,* a *Vespa* whirled past us so fast that the wind ruffled my curly, red hair. I pulled a few wisps away from my lips.

"Grams, I won't even be eligible to put my papers in for almost three more years. That's a long time."

Grams put her hands in the air and studied the clouds. "Oh sure, I guess that's an eternity at your age. It'll be here before you know it."

⟫⟩✦⟨⟪

We ambled through the stony, rustic town square to the *Duomo*. I leaned my head back and squinted through the sunlight in awe of the large antique Catholic cathedral with a domed roof. Grams pointed to her heeled, clunky, grass green sandals when Papa asked if she wanted to tackle the 642 stairs to the *Duomo*. Papa shrugged his shoulders and insisted I join him. He had a youthful look in his eyes. Half way up I wondered if this was such a good idea. Papa was breathing heavily in raspy breaths. We stopped to rest often and I offered Papa my bottled water. He had refused to bring any along saying he'd look "too trendy carrying *Evian*."

At the top of the cathedral, we had a bird's eye view of the whole, charming city. It was intoxicating watching all the tiny, European cars and scooters zoom by below. The people in the slow-moving crowds were barely distinguishable. People ebbed and flowed much like the tide of a sea. There were tall, rustic, stone towers and church steeples everywhere below us, and bells chiming periodically. Floral notes perfumed the air. A dog that looked like a small, caramel colored miniature walked around, stopping periodically at little green trees along the way. The scene below was bursting with life. Away in the distance, tomato-red tile roofs on buildings the color of sand dotted the rich, green rolling hills of the countryside.

As we snapped photos, I felt a cool breeze through my hair. The moment felt perfect and I was connected to my grandfather more than ever before. It struck me, with an empty feeling of dread, that he wouldn't be around forever. I grabbed a hold of his large hands, which had appeared mammoth-like in size when I was little, and interlaced my fingers with his. Papa had definitely taken my father's place when Dad ducked out of my life for a time. Papa looked at me and smiled. His eyes seemed to grasp my sentimentality.

"You look deep in thought. You all right there, Avie?" He placed his other hand on top of mine.

"Sure, Papa. It's just that it's nice up here with you. I feel happy. I want you to know, I really appreciate you. You've been there for me when others have not. I don't want to ever lose you Papa." My voiced quivered.

"Oh Avie, sweet Avie, I'm going to be around for a good long time, don't you worry. I take good care of myself." He patted his chest for effect. "Ship shape, that's what this ol' timer is. Peak form." He held up his arm and flexed his bicep muscle. I couldn't help but giggle. Then, he rested his elbows on the ledge and focused on the little world below.

"I hope Grams isn't getting to you too much," he said, studying the city. "She means well, you know."

"I know that, Papa. I'm used to it. Sometimes what she says does hurt, though." I leaned on the stone ledge next to him.

"I'm so sorry, Avery. She thinks she's helping you. I know it's a bad way to go about it. But still, I suppose her heart's in the right place."

"Are you guys happy, Papa?"

He chuckled. "You mean, because we're always nit-picking at each other all day and night?" He straightened up and stretched, with his elbows bent and his hands resting on the small of his back.

"I love your Grandma, faults and all. I know I'm not perfect either. But we do love each other. That's for sure. But loving someone, and getting along, well, that's a different story all together. This is how we've been for so long, it would be hard to change now. You can't take it too seriously. It's just how we keep one another in line. Love becomes complex over time, Avery."

"It seems like such a tough way to live, though, the constant spats all the time."

"Just lover's spats, Avery. That's all they are. Our love is rich and deep. It takes on many forms: contempt, anger, and frustration at times. But there's also admiration, endurance, joy and love. Nobody gets me going like Grams, even today. She's a feisty one, you know. I remember the first time I saw your grandmother. My word, she was gorgeous." I had never heard Papa speak this way. It made me a little heady. I couldn't stop myself from grinning.

He continued, "She had attitude, even then. As much as I

hate to admit it, that's what attracted me to her in the first place. We were at a church dance and she was telling the youth leader about how awful the punch was, and it really was terrible. All the other girls were sipping away with a plastered smile on their faces waiting for a gentlemen caller to come along. Not your grandma. Nope, Diane controls a room. It's never the same again, good or bad, you always know she's there. She's so full of life. I love her and I wouldn't change a thing. Don't tell her that."

I was intrigued and baffled to hear grandpa talking this way.

He continued, "Usually the very qualities you love about your mate are the ones that later sort of drive you crazy. But when you sit back and reflect, well, you really wouldn't change them one bit. Like I say, even if they do drive you nuts half the time."

I eyed Papa.

"Okay, most of the time. Even if she makes me miserable, I'm miserable in love, Avie. Miserable in love. How's that for a grandpa? Huh?"

We hugged each other close and I wished we could stay up there in the *Duomo* forever. Grandpa smelled like Scope mouthwash, sweat and aftershave. One of his pocket protectors full of pens pressed up against my chest as we embraced.

"It was Grams who talked your mom into letting you come on this trip," he said, almost in a whisper.

I pulled back from Papa.

"Mom didn't want me to come?"

"Nope."

"Why not?"

"Said you should be working a summer job to save up for college, that the trip was frivolous and unnecessary, stuff like that," said Papa.

"Wow, I didn't even know it was an issue."

"Yep, that's Grams. She fixed it. Her bark is a lot worse than her bite. She's always lookin' out for you, even when it doesn't seem like it. She's also the one who's talked some sense into your dad."

"What do you mean?" My heart felt like it leapt off the side of the cathedral.

"It's terrible how he disappeared and forgot all about you on account of his new wife and kids. She's badgered him, continually, until finally he's coming around."

"He's called me incessantly lately, right before we left Salt Lake. But I don't want anything to do with him, Papa. It's a little too late."

"It's never too late, Avie." He looked at me with his glossy eyes. "That's what Grams told your father. 'She needs you. She'll always need you. Don't continue to let her down her whole life. You've got to step up to the plate and bat. You work hard until she wants you to be a part of her life again. You crawl back begging if you have to.' When she said that to your dad, straight to his face, not a quiver in her lips, well, that might have been her finest hour," said Papa.

"I had no idea Grams was behind that. But, I'm not kidding though, Papa, I don't need him anymore, don't want him."

"Avery, it's important to give people a second chance. Even if a person doesn't deserve it, you owe God that much, to forgive, like He forgives you. Besides, you need your father more than you realize. You're just stubborn. After all, you are your grandmother's granddaughter. Right?" He was wearing a wide grin.

"I don't know, Papa," I put my hands up defensively in the air, dropped them at my sides and stared at the city below.

"Give it some time, Avery," he said after a while, as we walked arm in arm toward the ancient steps, in the refreshing breeze that was a nice break from the heat. "Promise me you'll give it some time. Time is the true healer of all wounds, that is, if you want to heal. It takes effort. And, it's a choice. It's always a choice."

Papa and I started our descent down the 642 steps of the

Duomo to the bottom where Grams was waiting for us, no doubt tapping her foot in frustration. Once we reached the ground level, he waved to her with two fingers, their traditional signal. She greeted him with a kiss and interlocked her arm through his. For the first time in the many years I have known them, I saw Grams and Papa in a different light. Our talk at the top of the *Duomo* helped me understand them more. I was amazed at the power of love, the ability to endure.

The day was giving way to night and the street vendors were rolling up leather belts, stacking purses, boxing unsold shoes and closing up carts, and finally, wheeling them away. I could hear the gentle clank of pottery as another vendor stacked the blue splattered bowls neatly and discreetly like she had done so many nights before. The whistles of trains and honks of *Vespas* were becoming increasingly faint as the town square became eerily silent. We headed back to our small hotel room. The street sweepers began spraying down the cobblestones, turning their matte finish into a lovely sheen in the last remnants of daylight. The dance performed daily here in Florence, and so it would be again tomorrow.

As we passed a bakery a large, smiling woman wiped her floury hands on her white apron. She flashed us a toothy grin while she pulled the shutters closed. A sweet, comforting smell from the pastries inside wafted through. I inhaled deeply, and felt as if I were home. How could this be when I was a gazillion miles away?

I sat down on the stoop of one of the shops that had just closed for the day. I retrieved the post card from my purse. I smoothed out a corner that was folded down, though the crease was indelible. I studied *Lucrezia's* face in the amber glow of the setting sun. I traced the elegant features of her face with my index finger. I wondered if she had lived long enough to know the complexities and endurance of love in old age, like Papa had spoken of? I smiled and wondered if she been so lucky.

On Sunday, Grams and Papa scoured Florence for a ward to attend. Enunciating every syllable and much louder than necessary, Grams asked confused locals, "Church of Jesus Christ of Latter-day Saints?" And then even louder, almost bellowing, "The Mormons?"

"Diane, they're Italian, not deaf, for goodness sakes," Papa said.

"Oh George! I've had just about enough of you this trip! Why, all I'm trying to do is get us all to church on the Sabbath! Is that too much to ask? To take our granddaughter to church while we travel? Really, George!" Grams slammed the bathroom door, shaking the ancient windows of our claustrophobic hotel room. The crucifix hanging over the doorway teetered but then, ultimately held its ground.

I suppose I had to admire their righteous desire to attend church regularly, even if they didn't always practice their religion on each other. I knew now that behind their bickering, true love still lingered unscathed.

The church service we found was well worth the trouble it took to find it. We wore headphones and listened to a young woman with dark, patrician beauty through the voice of a translator. Something about the process of having to concentrate on every word made God feel closer to me. So much effort went into every syllable, from the woman who was speaking at the pulpit, through the translator, and then to us.

It was strange seeing these foreign people with their dark hair, dark eyes and olive skin singing the hymns we sing back in Utah. It appeared most of the members were doing double duty, taking on more than one calling to make up for their small numbers. I noticed the same woman who led us in singing *Praise to the Man* in Italian also played the piano for the rag-tag choir's special musical number, and then she also taught Sunday school.

The talks were on charity, how we can emulate Christ by giving to and serving others. This simple theme struck me as vitally important. I felt heavy with emotion and inspiration. Grams must've felt the same way. I saw a tear roll down her cheek. She reached over and slipped her hand under Papa's, as was their habit. He smiled, the wrinkles around his eyes deep caverns of life's experience.

The congregation sang, *God Be With You 'Til We Meet Again,* which sounded much more exotic in Italian.

Though I didn't know it then, the pain I would face in the months and years ahead would be a refining process, working on my spirit like an alchemist works to turn baser metals into gold. There, in that humble chapel in Italy, I was receiving the keen instruction I needed.

After the service, Grams and Papa returned to their usual ways. When we got out of our taxi near the hotel, Grams whacked Papa with her pale pink purse. I smiled knowingly. I guess sometimes charity is easier to practice on people you don't live with.

⚜

It was our last night in Florence and I had mixed feelings. We were headed to Paris in the morning to visit the Louvre before boarding the jumbo jet that would take us home. As excited as I was for our brief stay in France, I carried a sense of dread in knowing that the trip was winding down. Once back in Utah, I'd be forced to deal with my future. I had no confidence in myself or my abilities.

Papa was still in the bathroom. I tried not to take note of how long he was always in there, but it was hard when we shared a tiny hotel room with two neatly made queen beds. With Grams' face strained and her arms crossed, I knew it was taking every amount of self-control she could muster to avoid saying, "George, did you fall in there again?"

I tried to play it cool, whistling a little happy tune as I looked out the window down to the busy people below, praying Grams would ease up on him. I didn't want to waste a moment of our time. I was already beginning to feel the unsettling and exciting feelings of change, a transformation within me that I would only later come to fully understand. Life is like that sometimes. We don't always get the lesson in the present. It's only in looking back that we realize how important each jagged stone was on our journey.

I buttoned the top button of my lilac cardigan sweater I'd thrown over my cotton shirt. The summer days in Florence seemed hotter than Salt Lake because of the humidity. The quaint city is just 100 kilometers from the sea. But like the Western United States, it cooled off nicely here in the evenings.

It's always good to dress in layers here. We'd been caught in a brief summer thunderstorm the day before, on our trip to *Pisa*. I learned the hard way that afternoon rainstorms are common in this region of Italy. Dripping wet, I had froze while we waited hours to find a taxi back to our little hotel. A surprising little storm had also caught us unawares coming out of *Giotto's Belltower* earlier in the week. Of course the weather was sunny and mild on St. John's Day, a national religious holiday, a day, we learned when absolutely everything was closed. We all took a long nap that day and I thought long and hard about my life at home. I had found that the downtime was a nice escape from their bickering, once I got used to Grams' and Papa's snoring in tandem, that is. I wrote a letter to my best friend Barclay. The rest of the day Grams and Papa had played pinochle and I browsed through the little gift shop, looking at post cards. I bought a few for Barclay, but realized that none could match the treasure I already had hidden in my purse.

So, while waiting for Papa, I made a mental note to ask the concierge, a crusty old man, for an umbrella on our way out. Papa opened the door to the bathroom and headed out, avoiding Grams' piercing gaze.

We took a short walk from the hotel and sat outside at a little sidewalk café called *Sostanza Delto 'Il Troia.* The lamplights burned and the rotund waiter with the large black mustache curled up at the ends greeted us, making me feel as if we had truly stepped back in time. I was hungry and couldn't get enough of authentic Italian cuisine. Grams rested her bifocals on the tip of her nose and looked menacingly at the menu before her.

"You'd think they could use more English in this country, why, it is, after all, the language. I mean really," said Grams, her eyes full of guile. "Just who do they think all the tourism dollars are coming from? Sheesh, you'd think they could cater to us just a little."

"Oh Diane, really now," said Papa, his tone soft, yet stern. "Would you please at least let them have their own language? We're in Italy, you know. Get it? We're on their turf!" Papa was so good at holding his tongue, a necessary skill through their fifty years of marriage. The few times he slipped, it always threw Grams. An uneasy, quiet tension ensued. I knew that, depending on Grams' response, the next twenty minutes could go either way, quiet resentment or an out-and-out verbal brawl. I was voting for the quiet resentment. My mom had felt the reverberations of their negative exchanges her whole life. I couldn't help but wonder how this had affected her and later, also influenced me. Did their negative treatment of each other inadvertently contribute to my negative self- image somehow?

"Have you decided?" the Italian waiter chimed in well-enunciated English.

Ignoring Papa for the moment, Grams spoke. "I must know, how did *'Il Troia'* get its name?" Grams' scowl changed to a cordial smile for the stranger.

"*Il Troia* was the name of the restaurant's first owner, a man who had the unpleasant habit of touching his guests while his hands were still greasy from cooking in the kitchen. He especially liked to touch the ladies. I guess he made quite an impression. So the name stuck."

Grams looked down nervously and straightened in her chair.

"Oh my," was all she could think to say.

Papa and I smiled at each other, knowing it took a lot to make Grams speechless.

Luckily for me, Italians truly know how to eat. The meal was an experience to be savored. It was clear Grams was still angry with Papa and embarrassed by her conversation with the waiter. Fortunately, the multi-course meal forced Grams immediately into the quiet resentment option.

The *primo* came right away; lovely fired pottery bowls of *al dente* pasta called *tortellini in brood*, in a clear broth that filled my spoon beneath the thick cheese-filled noodles. It was a far cry from the American Italian food I was used to. Back home, my mom would cook spaghetti until it was soggy and then microwave some tomato sauce from a jar to put on top. Even that quick meal was a rare occasion. The appetizer the waiter served us was the perfect accompaniment to the noodles, salty and smooth. I enjoyed eating in silence, grateful for a reprieve from their bickering, and the change of pace from the unsatisfying frozen dinners my mom had in the freezer back home.

From the patio, I noticed strings of white lights winding down the narrow streets, giving the city a sort of festive quality. A fleshy young Italian woman wearing a red dress with a long black braid down her back carried her baby boy in her arms, his head full of thick, black curls. We didn't have this kind of alluring culture in Salt Lake City. I was mesmerized just watching people walking on the streets. They looked so exotic to me.

The *secondo* was a grilled *fiorentina,* a prime wedge of meat lightly blackened. Papa had the same. It smelled divine. It was almost too much for my olfactory nerves to take in. When you don't ever swim in a pool you are overwhelmed at the sight of the sea. Grams opted for the grilled *sogliola,* announcing to the waiter in a loud whisper and pointing exaggeratingly at her belly, "Fish keeps my system moving much better than steak."

The waiter gave her a polite, forced smile.

I heard some giggling and talking in the distance. I noticed a tanned, stylish group of teenagers, most likely Americans like us, posing for a picture across the street. They were confident and a little shabby-chic with their thin cotton tees and cashmere sweaters tied at their waists. Funny how even here, seemingly a million miles away from West High, I could still feel so left out, so forgotten.

Our waiter was ebullient in announcing the *dolces* of the evening. He twisted the end of one side of his mustache into a fine point, his eyes full of light like he was truly inspired. Dessert was always my favorite part of any meal.

"I'll have the *tiramisu,* please. Can you make that light?" asked Grams. "Oh, I'm not so concerned about me, but my granddaughter, Avery, well, sweets just go right to her hips," Grams flashed a smile at the waiter and slapped my thigh under the table affectionately. I could have died. Papa gave me an empathetic look. This only made me feel worse about myself, adding on another thick layer of shame.

"Grams! Please! Why do you have to torture me like this?" I felt tears welling up in my eyes, along with the heat of anger in my chest.

"I'm just trying to help you, dear. Why, your mother always had the same problem, you know. Making good choices is the best way to diet, that's all. You should go ahead and have dessert. I mean, we can't really order *espresso* to top off our meal, like the Eye-talians do now can we? What would the Bishop think about that?"

Papa interjected, "*Tiramisu* has *espresso* in it, you know. And rum for that matter."

"It does? Ah, heck, if it can fit on a fork it goes in my mouth," Grams said with conviction. "That's my little rule. And if it's good enough for me, it's good enough for my granddaughter. Have some, Avie. But like I said, let's see if they can make it light."

The waiter bit his lip and shifted impatiently.

Grams turned to him and continued. "Doesn't she look like she could be in any one of those masterpieces in your museums? I mean really."

I winced and covered my face with my hands. "Grams, please don't."

Grams leaned forward, placing one hand over her heart. "No one back in the states appreciates her Renaissance look. In fact, did you know that she spent prom night . . ."

"I'll have the *crème caramel*, please," I interrupted.

I'd defy Grams in any little way I could, and use any means of avoiding going down that road again. The waiter smiled and turned on his heels, probably relieved to be almost finished with us. I wished I could have joined him.

That night back at our cramped hotel room, Grams and Papa debated the merits of trying to make it to an early Sacrament Meeting the next day before heading to the airport and traveling to France. As I lay in bed my last night in Italy, though I was tired and my feet were aching, it was difficult to sleep. My pillow was lumpy and both Grams and Papa were snoring. His was a high, throaty snore followed by a whistle in his nose. Grams' was more like a low growl or rattle with each breath during her deep sleep. Together, they created an odd timbre that made falling asleep difficult. Each night on our trip, I lay there for what seemed like hours, hoping I would eventually fall off to sleep.

My mind went back to *Bronzino's* beauty. How many handsome Italian men had muttered the name *Lucrezia* longingly? What kind of a life had she lived? What would my life have been like if I had lived back then? What if Grams was right?

But there's one person who thinks I'm beautiful.

"Like no other," Barclay would always say. "You're gorgeously unique. I've never liked the cheerleader type anyway, too boring. You've got character, Ave. That's more than I can say for most of those girls."

Barclay was like a brother to me, or so I thought at the time, before butterflies fluttered in my stomach at the very mention of his name. Then, he was just Barclay: my dependable friend, my only friend. He lived on my street in the Avenues, just five houses down. Both of our parents bought homes there when we were little, before it became the trendy place to live in Salt Lake. I remember meandering down I Street and playing with him at his house for hours on end. "I Street," what a funny name for a street right? I always wished it had been called something like "Apple Blossom Avenue." But no, all streets in the Avenues are letters of the alphabet. In some ways, wishing the name of my street was more appealing was symptomatic of my wish to be desired, looked up to and admired by others. If that's how you seek your self-image, by outward appearance, you'll never find it. If that's what you base your self-esteem on, there's always going to be something better around the corner. I was too foolish to understand that then.

Barclay's mother was elusive and a bit mysterious from the day I met her. But people were odd, to each her own, right? I would see her briefly on visits to his house. She was always in her silk robe and staring off into the distance. She would disappear into her bedroom the whole time Barclay and I played in his messy room. He would invent stories of his mother turning into a witch and flying away on her broom. I never saw his dad, but I knew he was loud and mean to Barclay and his mother. I guess they didn't mind him being gone so much. I thought it was just normal "adult fighting." After all, I'd been accustomed to it with my own parents before they split.

Barclay's room had orange shag carpet and stacks of children's books everywhere. His mom kept a rake in the closet to comb the carpet, though I never saw her use it or anything else in the house, for that matter. I never heard the whine of a vacuum cleaner and never saw her sweeping the kitchen floor. We loved to hide our toys in the masses of thin orange strands of the carpet in his room, pretending it was fire, pretending our teddy bears were screaming and trying to escape.

Once, Barclay kissed me on the cheek and told me he would love me forever. Did I know then what was to come? It was the first time I ever wondered about love as a little girl. While I suppose Barclay's feelings were just puppy love then, I remember how it struck me as odd that one day someone might actually love me, want to kiss me, for real. While exciting, the thought also made me shudder. Me falling in love with a man one day seemed about as likely as taking a little space shuttle to the moon, and about as realistic as me kissing Ken after riding Flicka together.

After he kissed me, Barclay went into the kitchen and made two messy cheese sandwiches for us to eat, with mayonnaise dripping over the sides. We both sat in silence and smacked our lips while we ate.

And that was that. We continued to be the best of friends.

During the sparse rainstorms in the summertime, we put on our bathing suits and played in his front yard. I Street has a steep incline, which made the gutters perfect for racing leaves in the current. We imagined they were boats taking us to faraway places. After the storm, soggy and cold, we would go to my house where my mom would make us hot chocolate from a mix she kept high up in the cupboard. We loved how she wrapped us up in warm beach towels she pulled from the enormous stacks of towels that she never threw away.

Mom's great in many ways, but I can still remember how her words that day stung like antibiotic eye drops.

"I can't believe you like hot chocolate in the summer time, Avery. It'll be 100 degrees out there again this afternoon as soon as the storm clears. You really should go for plain chocolate milk or even better, Kool-Aid, the special way I make it. You really don't need all this sugar. But whatever, at least I'm making it with low-fat milk." Mom leaned up against the green Formica countertop in her Capri pants. "And, I guess you and Barclay are having fun. It's all water under the bridge anyway." Mom had a way of using common sayings that never quite fit what she was talking about.

Even then, I remember feeling judged. I didn't dare ask for Kool-Aid because my Mom always made it without sugar. She said I had "pudgy tendencies" and wanted to help me keep it under control at a young age. The drink tasted awful, much worse than plain water. Whenever she gave it to me, it felt like a put-down you could drink. I can still remember the bitter aftertaste.

Judgment was something Barclay was used to, though. He and his family were not Mormon. Perhaps this is why Barclay and I bonded so closely and so quickly. He was one of the few on I Street who didn't attend the church around the corner. His strange mom and absent dad further ostracized him from the squeaky-clean families in our ward. People didn't intend to exclude him. It was just natural that all the Primary kids knew each other well and wanted to play together. The moms who sat together in Relief Society had an easier time making conversation on lazy afternoons outside before they put dinner on to simmer. Still, Barclay seemed to always feel forgotten. I guess that was our bond from day one. I had a soft spot for people who felt left out.

Even on Sundays, I would steal away, my knobby knees, my thighs rubbing together, taking me down I Street to Barclay's dark brown, two-story house. I would knock on his door our special way, two slow knocks and then two fast ones. This would let him know it wasn't the missionaries again, home teachers, or someone from the Elder's Quorum looking for his dad. Barclay would open the door with a grin, as if he was astonished to see me. I don't know why he always looked at me with surprise, or was it wonder?

Remembering those days made me miss my dear friend with an ache in my heart as we all sat in the hotel's coffee bar eating *brioches* and drinking fresh juice. The woman at the counter was slender and talkative, her large gestures exclamation points, clear in any language. She said with disbelief, "No *espresso*?" She looked baffled every time Grams and Papa shook their heads no. I noticed at the table to our left, an elderly Italian man sipping from a tiny white porcelain cup, returning it slowly to its diminutive saucer. A young couple sat close together sipping from their dainty cups, while he gently tucked her lovely and wild chocolate curly hair behind her ear. It must be intoxicating being in love in Italy.

I had never even had an official date, not one! Barclay had taken me to dinner for graduation, but that certainly didn't count. I remember we sat at the bar because there were no tables available. He's left-handed and kept bumping me while he ate. We sat there together in comfortable silence, not needing any words, and got up and switched places, so he would have some elbowroom.

I might soon be without my longest childhood friend, my only true friend, I guess. He was accepted to MIT and I was pretty sure he would attend school there in the fall. Why wouldn't he? He said that if I wanted him to stay and go to the U with me, he would. But I told him that was the silliest thing I'd ever heard. I couldn't imagine him giving up such a great opportunity, and for what? We were just friends. Though it would be painful, I was convinced that our friendship could last the time apart.

Grams and Papa had finished eating finally, and we were heading for the airport to board a plane for Paris. We waited outside the hotel for the shuttle, "to save a little money," Papa said. The wind was blowing, relieving the humidity and picking up the sweet fragrance of a bougainvillea. I suddenly felt sad to leave.

Two people were arguing, their rapid, taut Italian words audible in the distance. I was glad to have come face to face with the High Renaissance art my grandmother had talked about for so long, to stare into the eyes and see someone I recognized, someone who was revered in her time. I did look like them, the women in those 17th century paintings. This fact was clear to me now. That moment at the *Uffizi* Gallery was a turning point in my life. Strange how one event, one moment in time, no matter how seemingly innocuous, can change the course of your life.

As I helped papa sling our bags into the back of the van, I felt a sense of dread. There was so much to face back home: Mom, college, my dad's recent attempt to establish a relationship after there had been none. Still, as I got a glimpse of myself inside the shuttle in the driver's rearview mirror, I had the feeling that my biggest nemesis might be staring right back at me.

On the short airplane ride to Paris, I picked up one of the complimentary note pads that I found in the seat pocket in front of me. I dug for my purse underneath my seat, and I pulled out the post card with the painting of *Lucrezia* on it. As I looked at her, I put my pen to paper and wrote down some words that described my deepest feelings. Then, I lay my head back and fell asleep. When I awoke, the pilot was announcing our approaching landing. I crumbled up the paper on the seat table in front of me, put the post card back in my purse, and threw my thoughts away in the trash that the stewardess passed around before we landed. It was silly to write to someone I'd never meet. But I still couldn't put her out of my mind.

After a glorious day exploring the Louvre and catching a peek at the *Mona Lisa,* we boarded a transcontinental flight back to Salt Lake City. I'd purchased a small notebook at the gift shop. Once we reached our cruising altitude, and the stewardesses began serving sodas, I pulled out the post card again and decided to write her another letter.

I had plenty of time to compose my thoughts. It was a crazy moment at 30,000 feet, with the plane's engines lulling Grams and Papa to sleep next to me, where I tried to communicate with someone I had never even met, someone I couldn't possibly ever meet. I decided to keep this one. In an unlikely way, my letters to her would become my guide.

> *Dear Lucrezia,*
>
> *So I finally met you, one of the Renaissance beauties. You look so smug and distant in that painting. Were you trying to choose amongst your gentlemen callers, or debating the merits of chicken or fish for dinner?*
>
> *Grams' and Papa's heads are bobbing along with the turbulence that must be rocking them to sleep. This means that the tandem snoring that has plagued me this entire trip will now turn into public humiliation.*
>
> *I don't want to go home, though, either. So I'm sort of hovering in time here, not comfortable here on the plane, yet*

I don't want to face Mom. She never has anything good to say to me. I feel like I have no relationship with my dad.

I feel overwhelmed and sad to leave Italy. But you wouldn't understand that with your charmed life.

Avery

3

I dropped my bags on our cracking, brown linoleum kitchen floor. I was exhausted and headed for some milk in the fridge and some graham crackers from the pantry. The flight had taken everything out of me, and though it was morning here, I wanted nothing more than to collapse into my bed, shut out reality and remain functioning on Italian time. I knew my mom would be right behind me. She was parking the car in the garage.

While I poured the milk and got a few long crackers out of the package, Tigger jumped up on my leg and licked my hand, her tail flailing wildly. Good old Tigger, she was always happy to see me. Sometimes, I lived for my dog. She was just a pup the day I got her from the pound when I was nine years old. Tigger saved my life when my parents got divorced. I would lie on my bed and cry, and Tigger would lay her long, warm body alongside mine, never budging until I got up. She was faithful and loyal, and loved me no matter what. Why can't people be more like that?

I sat down at the kitchen table and dunked my cracker in my glass of cold milk. I raised it to my mouth where it dissolved perfectly on my tongue. Tigger sat on the floor at my feet and winked at me, an affectionate gesture she had done to me her whole life. I swear she winked. She was a mutt, a lovely mix of breeds that gave her some black, ragged stripes like a tiger. Her left ear was bent and her right eye had a white circle of fur around it. Canine perfection.

The crackers awakened my appetite that had been asleep from jetlag. I hadn't eaten anything on the airplane. I squatted down to pet Tigger, and stared into the refrigerator, noticing the stench of something spoiled, and then I saw several cartons of Chinese food that had been there since before I left. My mom: the quintessential pack rat. Our refrigerator was full to bursting, every inch of the shelves covered with cartons and jars of food. The items were stacked one on top of another so that reaching a soda became a strategic maneuver, a game of Twister. I closed the door, thinking I didn't need more to eat that badly.

"Ave. It's so nice to have you home," I heard my mom's lilting voice in the distance. "There's plenty of food in the fridge. Want me to fix you something? Those crackers aren't a very good breakfast," she said, replacing her keys on the hook on the kitchen wall.

"Hey Mom. It's good to be home. But no thanks. This is plenty," I said, lazily dipping another cracker in milk. "Nothing else looks good. I'd like to take a nap, though."

"Now, don't leave your stuff in the middle of the floor there like that," she said. "You know better."

Mom had on Capri pants, a wrap-around shirt, and way too much makeup. Smudged charcoal eyeliner lined her blue eyes.

"Mom, I've been home a total of 30 seconds. Could you please give me a break?"

She put her hands on her hips and gave me the look, eyes narrowed with hands resting on her hips, a gesture I had seen and ignored for many years.

"A penny saved is a penny earned, you know." My mom looked defiant.

"That makes no sense, Mom." Her clichés never made any sense.

Just as I stood up to go get my things and head for my room, she sighed and put her hands in the air, conceding. "All right. All right, Avery. You win. You can unpack later. I want to hear all about your trip. Tell me everything."

The metal chair squeaked as she pulled it out across the ancient, walnut colored kitchen floor.

"Mom, didn't you hear me? I'm tired. Can we please talk later?" I could feel my shoulders slumping and my traditional disdain rising. I was too tired to fight.

"Did you see the *Mona Lisa* at your stopover in Paris? Was it amazing? Breathtaking? What was your hotel like?"

"Yes, I saw *Da Vinci's* most famous portrait. I actually found it menacing, Mom. It's not at all what you'd think it would be. Really."

I sat back down, defeated, in a heap of fatigue.

"What do you mean menacing? That's a strange thing to say, Ave."

"Well, it's just that you think you know what the painting is all about, right? It's so renowned and you've seen pictures of the *Mona Lisa* tons of times, right?"

"Of course. I studied it in Art History at BYU, eons ago, before I met your father. If only I'd known then what I know now. It was for 'time and all eternity' then." Her eyes floated upward as she talked, as if she could see the moment years ago, she and dad standing there like the little plastic bride and groom on top of a wedding cake. Then, the cake she remembered came crashing down in her mind and her expression reflected it. "My how those plans can change," she said emphatically. "Anyway, what I'm trying to say is that I know my Renaissance art, Avery."

I could tell my mom was studying my hair with that critical look of hers. My hair had become frizzy on the long flight home. I dug for a hair tie in my pocket and instinctively smoothed my hair back into a ponytail.

"I'm sure you think you know all there is to know about the *Mona Lisa*, Mom. Everybody does." I rolled my eyes.

"No, everybody does not. Everybody doesn't get an "A" in a college art class. You think one trip to Italy suddenly makes you an expert? You think I don't know what I'm talking about just because I'm an executive secretary and not some lawyer or something? I was out of the work force for many years you know, taking care of you! So, now you're saying you're smarter than me?"

Her back was a stiff rod in the beat-up kitchen chair.

"I'm not saying that. You never listen to me, Mom. I'm sorry, but you really don't."

"All right, all right, Ave. What exactly are you saying?" My mom's eyes widened, her hands were splayed, she let out a long sigh and her expression was exasperation.

"What makes the *Mona Lisa* so amazing is her secret smile." I calmed my voice. "You see, she's got everyone fooled, Mom. *Da Vinci* is keeping her thoughts a mystery. He captures *Mona Lisa*, the subject he's painting, reacting to him. That's the genius of the work. Not all artists can do that. 'Infinitely subtle,' that's what the little thingy below the painting at the museum said. I always thought it was a self-portrait. But no."

"Avery, you're acting a little weird. Are you feeling okay?" Mom touched my forehead with the palm of her hand. "Maybe you're coming down with something, that weak immune system of yours. It looks like you didn't exactly eat healthily, honey, I can tell..."

I stood up, the squeaky chair sliding out behind me.

"Mom! I'm fine! I'm just tired! Okay? You would be too if you'd spent all night on a jet with Grams and Papa snoring!"

"Avery! Really! How ungrateful you are! Your grandparents give you such a gift for graduation and this is how you talk about them? You are unbelievable."

I grabbed my bags and headed for my bedroom. I had heard enough. Mom had a way of making me feel about two inches tall. This was record time, even for her.

"Leave me alone, will you please?"

I slammed my door and prayed she wouldn't knock. For once, my prayers were answered. In the quiet of my bedroom, I wondered if, like the *Mona Lisa*, there had been more to Lucrezia than the eye first finds, too. Could it be true for me as well? I resolved to dig deep to discover who I really was, to find strength of character, the subtle nuances of my soul that no one else could uncover but me.

My obsession began the next day. I went to the branch library in the Avenues. I walked inside the neat rows of bookshelves; the delicious, musty smell of thousands of books beckoning. A kind, heavy-set woman with a hunched back and thin brown hair cut in a bob helped me with my research. I couldn't get enough books, CD-ROMs and VHS tapes from the library about Renaissance Art. I sat at the polished wood table in the quiet reading room and dove into my treasures.

The more I read, the more I loved this period of art. Things are not always as they seem, and Renaissance Art is a prime example of that truth. I learned that *Michelangelo* came from a prestigiously wealthy family who was completely outraged when he decided to pursue art instead of a trade. He decided to try his hand at sculpture after believing he was a terrible painter. That feeling of ineptitude led to the celebrated *Statue of David*. Imagine that. He actually thought he had no gift with the brush. Yet his work on the *Sistine Chapel* has never been equaled. The strange looks on the faces of the young men he painted on the walls have bewildered scholars for centuries and awed tourists around the world.

I turned the thin pages of a large art book containing majestic pictures. I noticed a strange looking guy with greasy hair wearing a Grateful Dead t-shirt at the library's computer. His penetrating gaze was making me nervous. Two noisy, adorable little kids flanked their mom's side as she walked. She looked flustered and shushed them saying, "Library voices, please!"

I glanced at the clock and realized it was 3:00 p.m. I was supposed to be home right now so mom and I could "discuss my future." I would've rather had a root canal. I returned to my book and figured I would deal with my mom later.

The words on the pages before me seemed to speak to my soul. I learned that the time we call "The Renaissance" was about a new sense of what defined us as human beings. It was the first time people began to view human beings as Godlike, with grand potential. The art depicted humanity as dignified and responsible, suffering, but still standing and moving forward with life despite hardships. The artists of this time depicted people casting their own shadows, defining themselves, choosing their destinies. I was mesmerized. I could do that, too, couldn't I? Redefine myself? Carve out my own niche? Become comfortable in my own skin? Feel treasured though the world may not admire me? Maybe. But could I ever silence those negative voices in my head?

I closed the heavy book and rested my head on its cover. I thought back to the *Bronzino* beauty before me at the *Uffizi* Gallery in Italy. I had a window of opportunity here and I knew it. I sat up, opened up a smaller, thick book at the bottom of my stack. I had to learn more.

❧❧❧

I was two hours late to the little meeting my mom had planned and I was dreading the confrontation. I drove home in my mom's old Honda Accord, passing the tall quaint row of houses in our neighborhood. The sky was dark and rain peppered the windshield. I lived for rainy days. It always seemed to match my mood better than sunshine. The wet streets glistened and I could hear the splash of water in the gutters as I turned onto I Street. I noticed Barclay's ancient Beemer parked in his driveway, the one with lap belts only, which started up about two-thirds of the time. I felt a pang of guilt for having not yet gone to see him since I returned home from Italy. I'd sent him several letters and post cards from Florence, but that wasn't enough.

My mom was sitting in the living room when I walked in, next to the tall piles of magazines on the end table. This did not bode well for me. It was rare to see my mom sitting in there idle. She was always doing something. I called it puttering, which was basically defined as moving stuff from one place to another, making taller stacks of stuff to achieve the illusion that one was organizing. In her stillness she looked much gloomier than usual. She had dyed her hair a flat shade of black to cover the flecks of gray growing in around her face. The effect made her look like "gothic meets an aging BYU homecoming queen."

Mom clenched her jaw. "Where have you been?"

"I'm sorry, Mom, I was at the library and just lost track of time. Really, I apologize," I offered, shifting my weight nervously. Tigger ran up and licked my hand and panted excitedly, coming to my rescue, yet again.

"Lost track of time? That's your excuse? Do you know that I took off work today for you? I took off work, Avery. You know how hard that is for me to arrange with Mr. Blackwell. I'll have piles of work on my desk tomorrow. And for what, Avery? For what?"

"What else can I say? I'm really sorry, Mom, I didn't know this was going to be such a big deal." I headed for my room, Tigger at my side.

"Oh no you don't. You're not getting out of this one, Missy. Sit right down and let's talk this out," Mom stood up, she was pointing at me in a way that always made me cringe.

"Really, Mom, I'm so tired." I decided to try a diversion. "Hey, did you do something new to your hair? I really like it. It makes you look younger."

"That's not going to work, this time, either, Avery. I'm angry with you-- fuming!"

I sat down. "All right, let's have our little talk. My future, let's see…"

"Avery, stupid is as stupid does!"

"What Mom?" I shrugged my shoulders, put my arms out in a frustrated question mark. Tigger was squeaking now. She sensed the tension between Mom and me.

"I hate to say it, but you are so much like your father! You take me for granted and then leave me hanging all the time! I can't take it anymore." She buried her head in her hands and started whimpering.

I could handle almost anything from her, the ranting and raving, the misused clichés, and even the insults, but not the tears. I hated seeing her so vulnerable. It made me feel weak and guilty.

"Oh, Mom, I'm sorry. That's not fair. I'm here, aren't I? So I'm not like Dad, I'm not like him at all." I plopped down next to her on the couch and eased my arm around her slumped, trembling shoulders and continued. "I looked at the clock at the library, Mom, and thought maybe I could squeeze in a few more pages before I left. I realize now how important this is to you. I messed up again, didn't I? Can you forgive me?"

Her face was all red and the crying had turned into rapid sniffles now. There were black rings of mascara dripping in long smears down her cheeks.

"Our home teachers (sniff) are going to be here (sniff-sniff) in an hour (sniff). They will see what a 'happy little family' we are (sniff-sniff-sniff)."

"Mom, why don't you go take a warm bath. I'll go do the

dishes while you rest and then I'll light one of those good smelling candles you love. Candied apple? Or how about summer fruit? We'll be in ship-shape by the time they arrive. Okay? Mom?"

I leaned over to peer into her eyes, doing my cutest face, the one I knew she couldn't resist. As much as we fought, I knew I understood my mother better than my father ever did. These olive branches I offered would do the trick and we both knew it.

"Thanks, Ave. I appreciate that. Your dad's been calling you incessantly, by the way. He doesn't believe me when I tell him I've been giving you the messages. You had better call him back."

"What if I don't want to?" I asked.

"Do it anyway." Mom wiped the tear-streaked makeup from her cheeks with her fingers. "He wants to take you to dinner, says he has a graduation present for you."

"I don't want anything from him now." I scooted over putting space between my mom and me on the couch.

"Well, that's between you and your father. Oh, and Barclay's been calling you too, such a strange guy. But let's get back to the topic at hand. When can we talk about your major at the U?" She wiped her nose with a Kleenex.

"Over dinner. Let's order Sampan, that orange chicken is calling our name."

"Okay, Avie. You're a pretty cool kid, even if you do make me so mad some times," she rested her arm on my shoulder. "I don't understand why you're spending all your time at the library these days when you should be out in the sunshine meeting people, maybe going for a jog now and then? Really, Ave, you've got so much potential! I'm sure you didn't mean to make me angry."

"No, Mom, not at all," I said sardonically. "Why would I want to do a thing like that?"

The chapel was full that Sunday with light filling the small, arched stained glass windows with vibrant crimson, cucumber green, tangerine orange, and rose petal pink. My mom and I sat on a long wooden pew with the Paulsen family, all ten of them. Their oldest child was just thirteen. Two of the children elbowed one another playfully until one of the older kids whispered firmly for them to stop. A toddler sat wide-eyed, sticking his chubby fingers contentedly into a plastic bag full of Cheerios. I kept thinking about how, if our bench were a scale, my mom and I would shoot up into the air like a circus act, the weight of the Paulsens' eternal family much heavier with stability than ours.

Grams and Papa sat in front of us. Grams was wearing a loud, hot pink dress with dyed-to-match pumps. She had been bickering with Papa about something in a too-loud whisper through the opening hymn. I noticed Papa now had his arm around her, though, and she nuzzled comfortably to him. I smiled warmly with a new understanding about their arguments.

I turned around and saw my dad in the back of the chapel. His hair was slicked back, his face an amber tan. His expression, like always, was trying to mask guilt.

I had on my prettiest red dress, the one that tied in the back for the Sundays when I felt skinny. Mom always told me "red heads shouldn't wear red." Of course, this is probably why I always did choose a nice shade of scarlet. Besides, I thought it made my hair look like it was on fire next to my pale skin.

After the sacrament was over, the Bishop stood up to the pulpit. When he did, I felt my stomach drop to my feet, because I knew what was coming. I hated being the center of attention and I was not looking forward to the transition to Relief Society. They were announcing that I'd completed my requirements for a Young Women's award and transitioning into the ladies' club. I had gone into the meeting of women last Sunday and sat in the back with my mom. I had felt so uncomfortable. They were all just a bunch of mothers and old ladies. Who was I? Where exactly did I fit in? I tried to look invisible amidst the mothers nursing their babies, middle-aged women raising their hands to give wisdom, and elderly ladies shrinking together with dignity in the front row.

"This is a very special Sunday, brothers and sisters," said Bishop Aikin. He wore a preppy plaid tie, starched white shirt, and navy coat jacket. There were lines on his forehead. His graying hair was chopped in a neat crew cut and spiked up slightly with hair gel. "I have the honor, as your bishop, of placing the highest honor a young woman can receive in the church upon one of our Young Women at this time." He leaned on the pulpit as if it was a ship he was steering through a storm. "Today Sister Avery Rose will receive the Young Womanhood Recognition Award." Was he about to cry? Please, no! I thought.

"Sister Rose, could you please come up here and join me?" he said, wiping his eyes.

I stood up in front of the pew, straightened my dress and eased passed my mom for the long walk to the front of the chapel. I suddenly thought about how I'd rather be anywhere but here right now. As I saw hundreds of eyes looking at me, I heard a baby crying in the back and I wanted to join her.

The bishop leaned further into the microphone, too close, producing strong consonant sounds.

"I'd like to ask Sister Jamison to join us up here also, she's Avery's Young Women's president."

Sister Jamison, in her heels and perfectly-sprayed-in-place hair, walked down the aisle to the stand. I felt nothing for her. True, she always showed up to every activity on time and was there like clockwork every Sunday, always sitting in the front of our little Young Women's room with her presidency, often conducting. But I felt zero warmth from her. I always got the impression she was just doing her job and that she did not take any real interest in me. I noticed she was beaming as she stepped beside me.

"Sister Rose. Congratulations on your achievements in the Young Women's program," said the Bishop. He had one arm around me in a firm embrace as he spoke into the microphone. My palms were sweaty and my mouth felt dry. If my face were legible it would have read MORTIFICATION.

I felt Sister Jamison's soft arm around me on my other side. I thought I saw Barclay's mop of brown hair in the audience but how could this be? He buried his head in his hands immediately when we made eye contact. I never thought Barclay would show up. The years of feeling ostracized had built up hatred in him for the church. He had told me once that he would never set foot inside a Mormon church.

All these thoughts, and the weight of the many eyes on me, made me feel dizzy. The bishop put the gold necklace around my neck and shook my hand heartily. Sister Jamison gave me a token hug and then I quickly escaped, walking as fast as I could to my seat without tripping. I could tell my thighs were rubbing together and I said a silent prayer that the friction did not make any noise that was audible to the congregation.

Grams and Papa were wearing wide grins and tried to give me the eye as I hurried by them to my place next to my mom. If we turned out the lights, we'd still be able to see Grams' bright white teeth glowing, like the Cheshire cat. Plus, that dress she was wearing made my eyes hurt. What happened to the little old lady shawl? Not my grandma.

Once seated, Mom put her left arm around me and patted me gently. Her gesture of affection made me uncomfortable, it felt forced. How long had it been since we had hugged? It felt hot in the chapel and I could feel sweat in my armpits. I turned in time to see the back of my dad's slightly balding head as he left, shutting the chapel door silently behind him.

After Sunday School I wanted to escape the clutches of Relief Society. But my options were limited. Grams would want to sit together, all in a row, to show off "three generations of women" in the family. Mom would certainly make life difficult for me the whole next week if I tried to skip out. It was better to just endure.

The room was cold and rows of women in various heights of heels and sandals sat cross-legged singing *How Great Thou Art*. There was a painting of The Last Supper of Christ over the fireplace mantel at the front of the room. Grams had on a small, round, purple hat that matched her hot pink suit, shoes and purse. The effect was like an overgrown tulip. She turned and motioned wildly to me to sit between her and my mother, as if I wouldn't see them in the smallish room.

As I approached, she spoke in that loud whisper. "Hello, dear. Why, your grandfather and I were so proud of you today in Sacrament Meeting. I really didn't think your dress looked that bad."

That bad? What was wrong with my dress? Grams patted my back as I slipped by her to sit between her and my mother. I could feel the tension between the two of them, thick as water, as soon as I sat down on the padded folding chair. Mom was still singing the hymn enthusiastically but flashed me a between-the-notes grin. This was going to be one painfully long hour, I thought.

After the opening prayer and announcements, a tall, slender, blond woman stood up at the front of the room. She was wearing a stylish silk skirt and starched white ruffled shirt. Sister Dearborn was the new Relief Society President. I had seen her in the ward for the past few years but we hadn't really spoken. She was always busy with her young children.

"Welcome, dear sisters. I'm sorry to say that we as a presidency were negligent last week. We didn't introduce our newest member, Avery Rose," she said.

I felt all the blood rush up to my face, and I instinctively slumped down into my seat. Sister Dearborn turned toward me.

"Avery, we're blessed to have you here. I pray that your experience in Relief Society will be enriching for your whole life. May the Lord pour out his choicest blessings upon you," she said and smiled. There were faint wrinkles under her pale, ice blue eyes, and I felt a warm confidence rush over me.

But that fuzzy feeling didn't last long.

❧❧❧

On our walk home from church, Mom laid in to me about the dress I was wearing. That's how the fight started. Now it became clear what Grams had been talking about in Relief Society. Mom said it made me look bigger than I am. She said she'd been looking in magazines and noticing some great hair styles that would look so much better on me. I sped up my gait and put myself slightly out of earshot as we headed downhill to I Street. Too bad she had on her sensible shoes. She kept up with me, no problem.

"Bangs, Avery. That's all I'm saying. Consider getting some to cover up your high forehead." She was out of breath as she worked hard to stay with me, ignoring the obvious fact I was trying to lose her. "It just gets so shiny in the summertime, your forehead. I don't know why you insist on pulling your hair back. Some layers around your face would," she paused to take a breath, "thin out your cheeks, Avery."

Our pace was just plain silly now. She was practically chasing me. I'm sure our neighbors behind us got a good laugh watching the speed walkers in skirts and church shoes headed down the hill like clumsy racers.

I tried to pretend like everything was just fine. It was my

way of problem solving, a trait I inherited from a long line of people living in a state of denial on my dad's side: just tell yourself 'everything is fine' and maybe it will be.

The house was in sight. Once there, I would escape to the comfort of my room with Tigger. I would tell her everything, whisper all my troubles into her furry ear, as it twitched from the tickling of my breath.

I don't know what it was, maybe the endorphins from the aerobic walking, but I opened my mouth to speak and just couldn't stop. I turned to my mother and stopped abruptly. So did she. Words shot out of my mouth and I was above my body, watching this mean girl berate her mother.

"And I'm going to take beauty advice from a woman whose hair is such an unnatural shade of black that she looks like a Goth?" I asked, sardonically. "I mean really, Mom, you've never even had black hair in your life. Why now? Why, when you're starting to get old? And you're giving me fashion advice? You wear panty hose with sandals! That's so not stylish, Mom!" I resumed walking, ashamed of myself for how mean I was being.

I turned around and could see I'd gone too far again. Tears were welling up in Mom's eyes.

"You really hate it that much?" she said, reaching for her hair and slowly catching up to me. Her voice was timid. I loathed her tentative voice. It meant tears were soon to follow. She continued, "I just thought it would look, I don't know, striking." She ran her fingers through her hair and then wiped away a tear.

"Oh, it's striking alright, Mom. Striking out!"

At this my mom became engulfed in all out tears. It was officially a scene. I was certain the Pearsons were looking at us through their temple-like curtains from across the street. I knew I should back-pedal, apologize. My mom had been through so much with Dad leaving her for a younger, more attractive woman. But I was so sick of her criticizing me all the time. I just wasn't sure that I could make another peace offering. I took a deep breath and tried to do the right thing.

"I'm sorry Mom," I told her, placing my hand on her shoulder. "I didn't mean it. You look good. Great, even."

She waved me away at first and then looked up. Black mascara was running down her cheeks in two distinct lines. "Really?" She squeaked.

"Of course, Mom. I was just being belligerent."

"I'm sorry too, Avie."

We walked the rest of the way home in resigned silence.

⚜

That night, I went into the kitchen and made myself a tuna fish sandwich. I let Tigger lick the can clean. I poured a generous portion of Cool Ranch Doritos on the side of my plate and sat down on the couch, flipping through the TV channels. There was nothing interesting on. This made me even more depressed, just infomercials and re-runs, that's all I could find. There wasn't even anything good on Disney, though, technically, I was supposed to have outgrown this channel anyway. I cuddled up on the couch in my favorite cotton drawstring pants and opted for a little catnap, Tigger lying on the floor by my side. Then the doorbell rang.

I got to my feet and smoothed back my hair and thought fleetingly about not answering the door at all. Tentatively, I turned the knob and peered through the opening.

"Hello, Avery. I hope I'm not interrupting anything." It was Sister Dearborn. She had her hair back in a low ponytail and looked much younger than when she was all dressed up at church. Sometimes it's weird to see people out of context like this, like when you run into your schoolteacher at the grocery store. Tigger was panting and sniffing her ankles, her collar jingling.

"No. You're not interrupting," I said through the open door.

"Let me just put the dog away."

I closed the door on her for a minute and became a little panicked. What on Earth was the Relief Society President doing here? Was I in some sort of trouble? Had someone heard the way I spoke to my mom on the way home and missed the apology? Was this the ornery daughter police here to make an arrest? I led Tigger by her collar into my bedroom. Then I noticed my disheveled self in the hallway mirror as I headed back for the door. I looked sloppy and it made me self-conscious. The house was in even worse shape.

"Sorry, please come in," I said nervously.

"Thank you, thank you so much, Avery. Do you mind if I sit down?" I noticed she was already beginning to sit.

"Not at all, please." I motioned to the one empty space on the monster couch, named that way because it was so big, soft, old and engulfing. I sat on a chair at the other end of the room from her.

"Did you have a nice time with your grandparents in Italy? Florence, was it?" Sister Dearborn tried with futility to maintain balance sitting on the edge of the mushy sofa. Suddenly I felt like this was an inquisition. How did she know I went abroad? She must have sensed my discomfort, or she was clairvoyant.

"Your mom told me a little about your trip, kept me updated while you were gone." She smiled and I saw those lovely, kind lines.

"I had the most wonderful time." I crossed my legs and then uncrossed them. "We stayed in Florence, it was amazing, and then France on the way home. And the art, well, it's just breathtaking, really. You know, that's my grandparents' thing, I mean, taking each grandchild to Europe for high school graduation." I was now sitting on my hands to keep from wringing them.

"That must have been fantastic, and such a learning experience too. I'm so glad you got to go." I noticed Sister Dearborn was holding something. What was this about?

"Well, Avery, I can't tell you how happy I am that you're now in Relief Society. We are so lucky to have you." Sister Dearborn talked with her hands making little invisible circles and arches in the air. Her right hand was outstretched, giving subtle punctuation marks as she spoke. "Truly, you're a terrific addition to our group of sisters," she tucked her hair behind her ear and looked down, "Now, I know that the transition from Young Women to Relief Society can be a bit daunting. I bet you think we're just a bunch of mothers and old ladies, eh?"

"Oh, no, of course not," I fibbed, wondering if she really could read my mind.

"I want to do everything that I can to make you feel welcomed, Avery. I got you this book. It's by C.S. Lewis, it's called *The Screwtape Letters*. It's a funny title, I know, but the text is so thought-provoking. I think C.S. Lewis is the most spiritually in-tune, non-LDS writer of our time. I learned so much from this book."

She displayed the cover. It was a pale, innocuous watercolor painting that didn't seem to match the odd title at all. "It's the dialogue between one of the devil's assistants who is giving advice to his nephew about how to lead the human race astray. I think you'll find it very interesting."

Sister Dearborn handed me the thin book. I turned it over in my hands. Lewis was not a part of my entourage. I'd been carrying around *The Good Earth* ever since I got home from the trip. This shiny new book felt like a precious gift.

"Thank you. Really, Sister Dearborn, this is so nice of you."

"I just, I just want you to know I care," she said smiling. "I get the sense that this is an important time in your life, Avery. I don't know why, but I just do."

I felt a lump in my throat and my eyes got misty, but told myself not to cry.

"It is. You know, there's so much ahead of me, so many decisions, different paths I could take. It feels like the whole world is in front of me. That's daunting." I covered my mouth with my hand as I spoke, another nervous habit of mine.

"I'm sure it is, dear. You just have to remember that you're usually deciding between many good decisions, so really, when you think about it, you can't go wrong. It's what you do with the choices you make that might be equally important. You know, your attitude."

Sister Dearborn now took my hands in hers. I thought I would feel really uncomfortable with this physical affection, but I didn't.

"I also have a very important favor to ask of you, Avery."

What's this? A calling? I wondered. I drew my hands away. Is that what this was about? I furrowed my brow.

"It's not an official calling, mind you. It's just, well, Avery, a favor, a symbiotic gesture. I know there's someone in the ward who could really use your help right now. And I think the friendship just might benefit you, too. It's someone you've known for a long time." She dropped her hands back into her lap but kept her piercing gaze on mine.

"Who is it?" I was now on the edge of my seat, wondering who could possibly need me?

"She's struggling, Avery. The world has left her behind, so to speak. She is in the depths of despair and she really needs a friend. Do you think you're up for it?" She arched an eyebrow.

I nodded my head "yes." I really wanted to please Sister Dearborn.

"It's Katelyn Jamison."

What? I stood up, my hands on my thighs in exasperation.

"Her? The-most-popular-girl-at-West-High? You have got to be kidding me. She's hardly said two words to me, ever. She pretended she didn't even know me at school. I don't think she ever talked to me in Laurels. What could she possibly want from me?" I collapsed back down on the couch in a slump of disbelief.

"She's pregnant, Avery."

After Sister Dearborn spoke, the silence was deafening. We just stared at each other.

"That's right, four months along," she continued. "Her parents are beside themselves. They pretty much want to hide her because they're so ashamed, maybe ship her off to Idaho for the next five months. And all of her close friends have abandoned her. Katelyn is so down, I'm really worried." Sister Dearborn clasped her hands together, focused, as if she could solve the problem by using the right hand gesture. "She needs a friend, she needs you. This is your chance, Avery." She moved closer again. My mouth hung open. I was staring off into the distance, stunned. "This is your chance to do an act of true humanity, a real test of your character, being kind to someone who wasn't kind to you. This is your chance to show the world what you could become! And you might just save two lives in the process."

I wasn't sure if the "two lives" she was referring to were Katelyn and the baby, or Katelyn and me.

✦

All I could think about when I put on my tattered, comfy night shirt and pajama pants was how there was no way I could do what Sister Dearborn had asked of me. Anything seemed easier than befriending a perfect snob, even if she was in such a difficult predicament. And why should I even try? There had been so many times that I sat inside West High's cafeteria while all the cool kids sat out exclusively on the lawn. You had to be invited to eat out there, to that coveted large patch of greenery. It was an unwritten law of the school.

I always ate inside with Barclay. Often we would read our

novels to break up the silence and monotony, while we nibbled on thick, soggy French fries, dipping them in Barclay's own concoction of fry sauce. As I sat with *East of Eden* in my unzipped backpack next to me, we could smell the unmistakable aroma of the cafeteria, a mixture of peanut butter, white bread baking, catsup, and cleaning fluid. Just once, I would have loved for Katelyn Jamison, the popular cheerleader, to have come up and talked to me, maybe even invited me to sit with her. Still, I never really expected such a thing to happen. The lines were so clearly drawn in our school. Either you were popular or you were not. There was no in-between. Now, I was expected to help her? I didn't think so.

A part of me was glad to hear about her predicament. I supposed it served her right. Now, for once in her life, she might know what it felt like to be ostracized and forgotten for a while. Where was her big football-star boyfriend now? After all, she got herself into this situation, right? She could get herself out of it, too. I was sure she would not accept help from me, anyway. I would probably only add to her embarrassment. No, I would let her suffer alone. Let her wallow in her misfortune, let the scales steady for a moment and spread out the misery a bit. It was only fair. I owed her nothing.

I patted the empty space in my bed motioning Tigger up to join me. She looked at me as if to say, "Are you sure?"

"Come on, girl," I assured her. She snuggled in next to me and I turned on the lamp on my bedside table and opened the book Sister Dearborn had given me earlier that evening. I still hadn't spoken to my mother since our brawl on the way home from church. I could hear the low hum of the television set behind the closed door to her bedroom.

I noticed in neat cursive, Sister Dearborn had written a note to me on the inside cover.

Dear Avery,

I know that you are a special soul capable of greatness. May the words in this book inspire you to always try and do the right thing. Remember what Jesus Christ told his apostles at the Last Supper.
"A new commandment I give unto you, that ye love one another. As I have loved you, that ye also love one another. By this shall all men know that ye are my disciples, if ye have love one to another."
John 13:34-35

With Love,
Allison Dearborn

I read and re-read this scripture. True discipleship meant loving one another, even people who have done wrong by us in the past, even those who have sinned. I knew in my heart that I had to help Katelyn.

I turned the crisp pages and began reading. I found Lewis' words most intriguing. I had never considered gray areas in life that might lead me down a wrong path, something as simple as insulting my mother might mean I'm doing exactly what the adversary wants me to do. I'd never stopped to realize that I, too, might be difficult to live with at times.

It was chilling, in Lewis' depiction, to consider that there was a force out there working hard to make me do things that weaken me spiritually, so that the line between right and wrong becomes blurry and malleable. The weakening of self-control could lead to much worse things. I'd never considered this before.

In the book, C. S. Lewis wrote about the façade-like lure of transitory beauty, how beauty images change year to year, and are often impossible standards for a normal, healthy woman to achieve. I read Lewis' words:

As regards the male taste we have varied a good deal. At one time we have directed it to the statuesque and aristocratic type of beauty, mixing men's vanity with their desires and encouraging the race to breed chiefly from the most arrogant and prodigal women. At another, we have selected an exaggeratedly feminine type, faint and languishing, so that folly and cowardice, and all the general falseness and littleness of mind which go with them, shall be at premium. At present we are on the opposite tack. The age of jazz has succeeded the age of the waltz, and we now teach men to like women whose bodies are scarcely distinguishable from those of boys.

How would *Lucrezia* be viewed today? If she'd lived now and attended West High School, would she have been invited to eat lunch on the lawn? It was difficult to picture Renaissance women in cheerleading outfits, white knee socks drawing attention to their ample thighs. The thought made me laugh out loud, startling Tigger.

"Sorry Tigg," I said, patting her head. "Just cracking myself up a bit. Nothing for you to worry about. I think I might be going a little insane, that's all."

She looked at me and cocked her head, her bent ear falling down over one eye. Then she winked.

I read on, restacking my pillows behind me and taking the top cookie off of my Oreo so I could lick off the creamy, white frosting.

Despite the delicious treat, my mood was becoming black. I was tired and still upset about my mom. I started to feel anger rise up in me about Sister Dearborn. How dare she come and ask me such a thing?

It was ridiculous, the more I thought about it, discipleship or not. I'm a mismatched young woman, born in the wrong century, trying to find my way in a world that seems to be spinning out of control. How can I help anyone else when I can't even help myself?

 Dear Lucrezia,

 Tonight's letter will have to be short because I'm beat.

 You won't believe what the Relief Society president has asked me to do. She wants me to befriend someone who's been oblivious to me her whole life.

 We'd sit in the same tiny room in Young Women's and Katelyn Jamison would look off into the distance, rather than talk to me while we waited for our Laurel advisor. It's true! And now I'm expected to come to her rescue?

 My Mom and I had a major blow-out on the way home from church. Sometimes, I think I'm just one huge disappointment to her, to everybody. I know for a fact Barclay is mad at me for avoiding him. My dad's angry I won't call him back.

 My Renaissance books tell me that your era was about the artist finding the strength of character behind the ethereal beauty, that there had to be substance to their subjects, not merely outward attraction, in order for the painting to be truly magnificent.

 It makes me think that maybe I'm worrying too much about the wrong aspects of myself, the things I don't like about my appearance. Could this be a chance for me to prove myself, to decide who I really am?

 I would imagine your life was much less complicated than mine.

 Sincerely,

 Avery

4

The sun was blistering hot and the air was as dry as sandstone. During the short drive from the library back home, the air conditioner sputtered out cold, feeble air that was no match for the intense, desert temperatures. This was a particularly hot summer. When I coasted down I Street and pulled into our driveway, I saw the mass of brown hair that was Barclay. He sat on my front porch in his baggy jeans with his elbows on his knees, letting his long bangs completely cover his eyes. His head was down, studying some imaginary pattern on the pavement.

I waved in his direction, but he didn't look up. I stopped the car and yanked the parking brake into position and grabbed my cumbersome bag full of Renaissance books. Today they felt heavy, as if I were carrying the weight of 400 years of moral development.

Barclay wore a sullen expression. I decided to use the same trick I always tried with my parents when they were fighting and pretend everything was fine.

"Hey Barclay! How are you? I've been meaning to call you," I beamed. "Really, I have. I've missed you." I plopped my clumsy book bag down next to him and sat down, touching his shoulder.

He peered up at me through his uneven, curly mop. I saw anger and pain in his eyes. I knew Barclay had a dark side, nurtured for many years by his cold and distant mother.

"Barc," I shook him gently. "It's me, your favorite redhead. Asking for mercy? C'mon didn't you miss me? Barc? Listen, I'm sorry I didn't call sooner. Really, I am. There's just no good excuse for that."

I saw a sweet little grin break on his lips. I knew he couldn't be mad at me for long, even if he tried.

He wrinkled his forehead and his bushy eyebrows. "Avery, don't try to get out of this. You've been home two weeks now and you haven't even stopped by. What's the deal?" He stood up abruptly.

"Barc, I said I'm sorry," I stood up next to him, facing him, my hands outstretched. "It's just been crazy, there's been so much going on. I've been trying to recover after being in such close quarters with my grandparents on the trip, you can imagine." I forced a laugh but he didn't crack. "I mean they're great and all, and I really understand them better now, but still."

I drew a little 's' with the toe of my sandal in the dirt in the flowerbed next to the porch while I spoke. "I'm dealing with my Mom, you know, the usual. And you wouldn't believe what the Relief Society President is asking me to do. Oh, and on top of all of that my dad won't stop calling and I don't want to talk to him. I'm just feeling so low about myself these days--"

"What about me, Ave?" He interrupted. This was not like him to be rude. His boldness took me aback. "What do you suppose I've been up to this summer? Oh just a bundle of joy over at our little family 'love hut.' Yep, that's it. My mom's been in bed for four days straight, yep, don't even know if she's eating. It's pretty bad this time, Ave. Do you think I should call someone? If so, who? What would I say? 'Um, hi, my mom's crazy. Can you help me?"

He started walking toward the street to head home, jerking the hair out of his eyes and sticking his hands in his pockets with his slouchy walk, his usual gait that always reminded me of the cartoon character "Shaggy" from Scooby Doo.

"Wait a sec, Barc. I didn't know, really I didn't. I'm so sorry," I followed him, wringing my hands nervously. "That's terrible. What can I do? How can I help you out?"

He turned to me. I could see beads of sweat on his forehead through his mass of hair. His t-shirt was wet with sweat on his chest. "Try being there, Ave. That's all I ask. You know, being there for me like I am for you. Is that so hard?"

Even when he was angry, there was something adorable about Barclay. He was like a puppy dog. He clenched his jaw, narrowed his eyes, but something behind them told me he loved me dearly.

"Forgive me?" I smiled. "Please? Old buddy, old pal?" I punched him mockingly in the arm. My grin widened. "Barc? I'll make it up to you, I promise."

"I don't know." He turned with me toward the house. Instinctively, we walked toward the door together, without saying a word. Once inside, I gave him his favorite IBC Root Beer. I popped open a key lime soda for me while Tigger licked my toes and then panted her way over to Barclay to say "hello." Barclay was the only other human being she liked nearly as much as me.

"I was there you know," he mumbled, his back to me sipping his soda as he sat on the overstuffed, brown sofa monster.

"Where?" I asked, moving toward him, moving a stack of books and papers on the couch. There was an even larger pile on the end table to my right. Then, the large, soft cushions of the couch consumed me as I sat down and sipped my refreshing drink.

"At your church last Sunday," he continued. "Your mom mentioned that it was a big deal for you. She told me about it when she was out for a walk one morning while I was weeding the yard. She said it would mean a lot to you if I came. So I was there," he said, waving his hand in the air. "I guess you didn't see me." Barclay took a long draw of his root beer.

"I saw you. Couldn't believe my eyes, but I saw you. There were so many people staring at me while I was up there. You know how I hate being in front of people, it's so embarrassing." I screwed up my face sideways and squinted, wishing the memory of it away.

Barclay touched my shoulder gently. He looked up at me. "You looked really pretty, Avery," his eyes flashed down at the Berber carpet. "You did, Avery—looked so nice up there, I mean. You always do."

"Thanks, Barclay. I, I don't know what to say." My face felt hot. I was blushing. "And thanks for coming. I know that was a big deal for you. I really appreciate it."

He turned to me and then he smiled. Holding his IBC between his knees, he scratched Tigger behind her ears.

"There's not much I wouldn't do for you, Ave, you know that," he said, without looking up. I reached into my purse and touched my precious copy of *Pride and Prejudice*, running my fingers across the edges of the pages with my thumb, like a card dealer shuffling his deck of cards.

"You still do that?" Barclay asked, smiling.

"Do what?" I was playing dumb.

"Carry around novels you've already read a bunch of times just so they can keep you company?"

"Yes. I guess I do." I studied the floor. Barclay didn't know that I carried *Lucrezia* in the pocket inside my purse and that I wrote letters to her regularly. Even he might find that a bit insane.

"I know you so well," he said, chuckling. "Any Hemingway in there?"

I smiled weakly and shook my head. "Just a little Jane Austen and a Faulkner or two."

"Ah, of course. I should've known." Barclay's eyes were bright and he smiled so broadly that his dimples showed.

I could tell I was blushing again.

"It's okay, I think it's cute. Your books are your friends," he explained, putting his arm around me. "What better friends can you have? A good novel never disappoints you."

"No, I suppose not."

"You're a unique individual, Avery Rose." Barclay studied me like an antiques collector picking up a rare, hidden find. "Truly one of a kind. I wouldn't change a thing about you."

Barclay was all sweetness most of the time. I really felt for him, his parents had put him through so much. I wished others on our street would've tried to reach out to him more, tried to make him feel like he belonged at least a little bit. His happiness was a heavy load for me to carry by myself.

Barclay and I spent the afternoon together and it felt good, just sitting there and chatting. Then we watched TV for a while. I'd almost forgotten how easy it was being with him, so serene and effortless, like floating in a turquoise pool on a warm, sunny day.

My mom was still gone. Where was she? I was actually relieved that I didn't have to deal with her, though I was a bit worried. I also wondered if my apology hadn't been enough, if I'd crossed a line and gone too far with my insults this time. Even though she'd apologized too, the wound was still open and at risk for infection.

❧❧

Barclay left later that evening. I checked my voice mail messages. I pressed "2" to "retrieve new messages" and heard the unmistakably soothing voice of Sister Dearborn.

"Hi Avery. This is Allison Dearborn calling," her voice as rich as molasses. "It was so good to see you last night. Listen, I wanted to give you Katelyn's phone number in case you don't have it.

It's 4-8-5—8-1-2-0. It would be good if you could give her a call. Just check up on her, Avery. She needs a friend. Thanks so much and I'll see you next Sunday."

I replayed the message and grabbed a pen so I could write down the phone number and then I crumpled the paper and shoved it into the drawer.

Then I listened further, to the polite, monotone voice mail woman's voice telling me I had another new message.

"Hey Ave, it's me." It was my dad. "Why haven't you returned my calls? I'm sure your mother hasn't been giving you the messages again, typical of her. But sweetie, I want to see you. Can I take you to dinner, say tomorrow night? The kids are getting so big. They really want to see you. I want to hear about your trip to Italy. Call me as soon as you can, A-S-A-P. All right, talk to you soon. Bye."

❦❦

The door shut with a soft click behind me. A mass of auburn hair cut in layers with strawberry blond highlights stood before me. It was my newly coifed mother, at least I think it was, she looked completely different. She threw her keys down on the counter and walked past me toward the fridge for a Diet Coke. The silence was awkward. She walked purposefully, avoiding my gaze. I loathed our long stretches of emotional distance and seethed with years of anger and hurt feelings.

She ambled over to the pantry and opened up a bag of Tostitos and crunched them quietly while sipping her can of Diet Coke. I saw her open up the top envelope in one of her stacks of mail. Mom eyed the bill menacingly, as if it was her enemy. She seemed oblivious to the fact that I was standing right there, waiting expectantly, for her to say something, anything.

"Um, hi Mom." I stepped closer. "It's me, you know, your only child?" I waved my hand in front of her face unable to control my inner brat.

"Hello Avery," she said, icily, without looking up.

"I like your new do, Mom." I leaned up against the counter top, pretending, as always, that everything was hunky dory.

"I surely didn't want to look like a Goth any longer, now did I? Satisfied?" She threw down the mail, hitting another large pile that scattered in a messy heap.

"I said I was sorry, Mom. Things got out of hand that day. How many times do I have to say I'm sorry? I thought we were over that." I was wringing my hands.

"I thought we were too. It's just been hard to forget the things that you said, Avery. I work so hard to try to stay looking good. It gets harder to do, you know, as you get older. I just didn't need to hear those things from you. You have a sharp tongue sometimes." She turned to me and stared directly into my eyes with a piercing gaze. Her hair was the color of fire. "You don't respect me like you should. You saw your father walk all over me and you've always thought you could do the same. A doormat, that's what you think I am."

The silence was turning to anger. Well, that, I could manage, bring it on.

"Mom, take it easy. What's the deal here?" I snapped back. "You weren't exactly being nice to me with your usual cadre of insults." I folded my arms and stared right back at her.

"Cadre of insults?" She said in a mocking tone. "What is that, a new college word? I'm so impressed, Avery." She began to walk off.

"Mom! I'm sick of it too, to tell you the truth. All the insults, all right? You are too hard on me." I forced myself to calm down and lowered my voice. "You always have been."

"I'm not hard on you." She shot back. "What? Trying to help you? That's all I have ever done Avery. You're so ungrateful."

"It's the way you say things, Mom, about my hair, my dress, my thighs, my weight. I'm just never quite acceptable to you. I'm just one big disappointment to you. It hurts me, it really hurts."

"Oh please, Avery." She dismissed me with her hand, checking out her new hairstyle in the hallway mirror as she walked past. "Now you're just being too sensitive, which is ironic. You sure know how to dish it out."

She slammed her bedroom door.

"Mom!" I pounded on her door with my fist. "Mom! Open this door! I'm not finished!" I pounded some more.

Silence.

Then I said those three awful words I would later regret. No child should ever say that to her parent.

"Mom! I hate you, Mom! I really do! Do you hear me! I hate you!"

I ran to my room and slammed the door behind me. I threw myself down on my bed and sobbed. Why had I decided to stay here and go to the U? My decision had been a financial one. I reasoned that it would be cheaper paying in-state tuition and living at home. But at that moment, because of my pain, I thought that working three jobs while attending classes out of state would've been better than living here, enduring this regular torture. My head was spinning.

Tigger was squeaking for me to let her in, which I did.

"Always to my rescue, aren't you Tigg?" I said, choking back tears. I stroked her rag-tag, striped fur. "I thank God for you, Tigg. I really do. Everybody needs a loyal friend like you."

This thought struck me. I lay back on my unmade bed with sheets askew and stared up at the ceiling. As much as I tried to deny it and think about something else, I knew exactly what I had to do in the morning.

The clock on my bedside table said 10:00 a.m. Tigger was still slumbering next to me peacefully. I felt groggy and heavy as a rock. Lifting myself out of bed felt like a laborious chore. The second I sat up so did Tigg. She appeared immediately ready for the day. I slipped on my drawstring pants under my nightshirt and yawned. I limped into the kitchen, barely awake, and found my mother dressed for work, reading the morning newspaper and waiting patiently for me at the kitchen table. The sight of her, usually gone by this hour, made me jump a little.

"Did you sleep well?" Mom asked.

"Yah, pretty good, thanks. Shouldn't you be at work by now?" I asked around a yawn. Then I stretched and rubbed my eyes.

"Yes, I'll be in big trouble I'm sure." Mom rolled her eyes. "But I just couldn't leave the house before making things right with you."

I pulled out a chair and sat across from my mother. She told me tenderly how much she loved me and that she was sorry that she had hurt me. I apologized to her as well and assured her that I didn't mean those horrible things I said last night, or that Sunday after church, and that I loved her too.

We hadn't always been this way. We were best friends when I was little. I remember when mom lit the candles on my cake for my 13th birthday. She cringed and said, "A teenager! Oh no!" We laughed, and I took a deep breath and blew out all of the candles. I remember thinking, *I'll be different and not your typical teenager. There was nothing to worry about.* We were inseparable when I was in kindergarten. After school, I'd walk outside and search the rows of cars for her and begin running toward her as soon as my eyes found her. She'd put her car in park and climb out of the driver's side to give me a hug before opening the back door for me to get in. On lucky days, when I'd been extra good, she'd go through the drive-through at a fast food restaurant on the way home and buy me a chocolate milkshake.

Even after Dad left, it wasn't as bad as it was now between us. Though I had blamed Mom for Dad leaving us, that didn't stop us from clinging to each other. We'd rent movies and cuddle up on the monster couch with a large bowl of buttered popcorn. While we watched, we'd let our bare feet touch, my little foot resting on top of her toes. Usually, my eyes would grow heavy before the movie ended. I'd put my head on her shoulder and then later, find myself tucked neatly in my bedroom when the morning light appeared through my window.

I wanted to change the way things were with us now. I told myself that I could do better, and then each time I'd let my temper get the best of me.

"Bye, sweetie," Mom said, grabbing her briefcase and slinging its strap over her shoulder.

"Bye Mom. Have a good one."

She thanked me and I heard the door click shut behind her.

I plopped a can of orange juice concentrate into the plastic pitcher and stirred while I stared blankly out the window at our parched, yellow grass. The lawn was like hay. The yard was always the first thing to go when Mom was having a tough time. Dad had always done the mowing and watering. For years after their divorce she let the yard go completely to weed as a subconscious rebellion, much to the chagrin of our neighbors.

Green, neatly manicured lawns line our sloping street. The state of one's yard was an unspoken status symbol. The lush mowed lawns with brightly colored flowers outlined in concrete curbing and filled in with fragrant wood chips said to the world, "Hello, we are doing well." And then there was ours, flaxen and dry. The only green was the stubborn, die-hard weeds pushing up through the concrete. We might as well have shouted to the neighbors, "We're miserable here!" Mom had made an effort to make our yard on I Street presentable. But she still neglected it whenever family problems arose, as if the yard were a litmus test for our dysfunctional lives. The neighbors could take one look at our yard and tell exactly how we were feeling. Today our yard was a blow horn broadcasting that we were wrung out, betrayed, angry and forgotten. Maybe she'd turn on the sprinklers when she got home. Our lawn thirsted for water, like I had longed for the chat we had this morning.

I didn't want to face the task that lay ahead of me thanks to Sister Dearborn.

The glass of orange juice in my hand tasted too sweet and the sugar went straight to my head. I tried to balance out the sweetness with some hearty Grape Nuts cereal and skim milk. Then I dug into our "everything drawer" for the little slip of wrinkled paper where I'd scribbled Katelyn's phone number. It took some digging, amidst about a dozen receipts, batteries, numerous pens, rubber bands, pictures from our trip to Disneyland years ago, and a ward directory that was ten years old.

I found the crumpled piece of paper. Just holding her phone number in my hands made me feel nervous and edgy. Sister Dearborn had obviously misjudged me. I wasn't that strong and certainly not this selfless. Still, I suppose I had to try.

I put my bowl on the kitchen floor and let Tigger lap up the remaining milk in the bottom while I picked up the cordless phone and dialed. There was no answer. I put my finger on the blue button to hang up the phone when I heard a muffled voice in my ear. It sounded as if I had woken someone from sleep.

"Hel-lo?" The soft, raspy voice said.

"Hi. Is Katelyn there?" I asked.

There was an awkward, long pause. I considered just hanging up altogether. This was a mistake, I thought. It wasn't too late to abandon this futile plan.

"Hello? Is anyone there?" I asked.

"This is Katelyn," a weak voice responded. "Who is this?"

I steadied myself with my hands on the Formica countertop.

"Hi Katelyn. It's Avery Rose. From the ward, your old Laurels class?"

There was another pause.

"Why are you calling me?" Her voice was strained and quick.

"Well, I—I . . ."

"Am I everyone's charity case now?" Her words were verbal darts in my ear.

"No, not at all." I stammered. This was going to be even more difficult than I had imagined. I regretted calling her in the first place.

"What is it, then?" She demanded, her voice taut with defensiveness.

"I just wanted to see how you were doing," I offered. "I wanted to, well, see if there was something, anything, I could do for you." What was the protocol for this? I closed my eyes and berated myself for sounding like such a dork.

"Why now, Avery?" There was mocking in her voice. "You've hardly talked to me in the past. Why now? I'm not interested. Just go hang out with that weird friend of yours Barclay."

Now my fear was turning to anger. She had crossed the line in attacking Barclay. It took all my self-control to remember my goal. The only way I managed this was by picturing how I would feel in her shoes. I summoned some sort of strength I didn't know I even had.

"I just thought you might feel a little lonely right now. I know how that feels, to be sort of alone. I guess I just want you to know that I'm here and that I care." I winced as if I'd just touched something burning hot, expecting the recoil of her rejection.

"I do. But why should I talk to you about it?" she said. "I mean, I always thought you hated me."

I gasped. "Hated you? I thought you didn't ever want to be seen with a dork like me."

"No, not at all," she said. "I would've loved getting to know you better. The way you looked at me, I thought you wanted to be alone or with your best friend Barclay."

I waved a dismissive hand in the air. "Quite the opposite, I always longed to fit in. I thought there was some sort of unspoken rule that you had to be invited into the group."

It got awkwardly quiet again. We seemed to always come back to this. We weren't going to get anywhere debating the politics of high school. I decided to take another approach.

"Do you like animals? I could bring my dog Tigger by. She's really cute."

"I love dogs. But I don't know. I don't really want to see anyone. My mom is allergic to dogs so I've never been able to have one. Wait a minute, why not? My mom and I haven't been getting along lately anyway. I can't do anything right these days. Why try? Go ahead and bring Tigger over."

"Is this afternoon okay?" I braced myself again for her to turn me down.

"Yeah, I suppose so, maybe, that should work. I'm really not up to my social graces right now, though, I have to warn you. Everything really sucks for me. I've already gained twelve pounds. Twelve pounds! And that's the least of it, really. I dunno what I'm going to do. It's just awful. I never imagined I could be like this, you know, pregnant at age 18, like some big fat loser. I had so many goals."

"Hey now, don't talk that way. All right?" I said. "I think my dog Tigger actually really likes 'pregnant losers.'"

She laughed and I instantly felt a wave of relief. I couldn't believe she had already opened up to me so much.

The knock on my front door later that morning was loud and persistent. I knew it was Barclay. I was reading the newspaper, trying to pass the morning. I bounced over to answer it. Tigger was following close behind, grateful for the diversion. I swung open the door and it startled me to see my dad standing there. I had been expecting Barclay's mop of cinnamon brown hair.

"Hey, Avery. I've been calling and calling you. How are you, sweetie?" He walked inside comfortably, almost like he still lived here, though it had been nine years since he left us. He was unshaven but well dressed in a pinstriped suit and pale blue tie.

"Hi, Dad. Won't you come in," I said to the back of his head with sarcasm on my tongue.

He inspected the stacks of books, newspapers and mail around him in the living room. "I see your mother hasn't changed." He rolled his eyes.

I wouldn't play this game. I had been subject to the tug-of-war between them for far too long.

"What do you want, Dad?" I stepped back from him, putting a safe distance between us. At this, his facial expression dropped.

"What do I want?" he repeated. "I'm here to see you, sweetie. That's all. I've missed my girl. It's been months since I've seen you." Dad sat down on the billowy sofa. The depth that he sank to seemed to surprise him and I had to stifle a laugh. How could he have forgotten about the monster couch? "What's going on, Avery? Why are you avoiding me?" My father was trying to stay composed while being completely enveloped in the sofa. "Why are you upset with me?" He struggled to get up and reached for the bag of pretzels on the coffee table.

"Oh, I don't know, Dad. Why don't you take a guess?" I watched him douse a pretzel in the cup of ranch dip I'd gotten out of the refrigerator earlier. He's the one who introduced me to this decadent treat. The salt on the pretzels was even more pungent with the creamy dressing. The combination was sumptuous.

His mouth was full and he was crunching in between words. "What? Did I say something that offended you, Ave?" Dad licked his fingers.

I grabbed for a pretzel and dipped it in the creamy dressy. "I've just been busy, Dad. I do have a life too, you know. Why do you get to call the shots on our relationship?"

He dove in for more of the mouthwatering snack. I wasn't sure if I wanted to get into such a deep discussion with him. But, I supposed I had no choice.

"What do you mean: 'call the shots?' I just want to know my daughter, is that too much to ask? I'm sure your mother has filled your head with things about me, but they're not true, Avery. Simply not true."

"I know what is true, Dad. You were busy with your new family all during high school. Missing in action, that's what you were to me. And those were some tough years, Dad. I needed you." I started to cry a little and hated myself for losing control so easily.

My father shook his head and bit into another pretzel, seemingly unaffected by my show of emotion. "Yeah. I remember. Stupid boys."

"You don't have to remind me, Dad." I stood up hoping to escape to my room.

"Not so fast, young lady. You stay right here and talk to me." His stern tone turned me into an eight-year-old girl again. I was frozen there midstep, I couldn't move. "I'm sorry, okay?" His tone softened as he stepped toward me. "I know I've made a lot of mistakes in my life and choices that are difficult for you to understand. I'm sure it has been no picnic for you."

"That's a major understatement, Dad." I turned away from his gaze and stuck my hands in my pockets.

My father took a step closer and I could smell his Old Spice. I wanted to bury my head in his stubbly neck.

"How long are you going to punish me?" He pleaded. "Huh? How long must I suffer for falling in love? For finding happiness?"

"Happiness? What were we, Dad?" I was half shouting, half crying. "Just a practice family?" I grabbed my keys and ran out the front door to my clunky car in the driveway before he could catch me. As I sped off I could see him standing on the haystack lawn looking my direction, pleading. At that moment I felt like I never wanted to see him again, just drive, drive, drive. There was so much hurt. I put my foot on the pedal and both hands gripped the steering wheel. My old car caught its second wind, catapulted up I Street, and I was gone.

Dear Lucrezia,

I'm sitting here in the Foothills of Salt Lake City overlooking the city below me. It looks miniature from this vantage point, as if all the cars were toys and the busy people mere figurines. Sometimes I wonder what life is really all about. I wonder just who is calling the shots? Are we all simply fools in this game called life? Sometimes it all seems so pointless.

The rock I'm sitting on feels like a stovetop in this midday heat. I won't be able to stay here long. I have a strange appointment to keep. I'm going to visit a girl from my church class who was much like I imagine you were, beautiful, admired, and popular. All that has changed drastically for her now, though. She's pregnant and not married. In fact, her high school boyfriend, the baby's father, isn't even talking to her anymore. College, I guess, is out of the question for her at the moment.

Am I terrible, because at first I was glad to hear about her predicament? Her life has always seemed so perfect and I have been envious. It seems I can't get through a day without fighting with my mom. I don't know why I'm so harsh with her. My dad traded me in for a new family. My best friend's mom is in the throes of a major depression.

Look at me right now, sitting on a rock, in the Foothills of Salt Lake City, writing to a woman who has been dead for centuries. And I'm headed to visit a person I have nothing but hatred in my heart for all because the Relief Society President came to see me. There's no telling what will happen next.

Yours,
Avery

5

The glossy and ornate black door was daunting. Tigger squeaked at my side, impatient and anxious. I tightened my grip on her leash. The hot wind on my back was blowing my white linen shirt up in billowy ripples. I knocked again. The silence confirmed what I'd suspected all along. Katelyn Jamison didn't need me and I certainly did not need her.

I turned around to leave and decided to stay there for just a few more minutes. Once I left, I knew I'd never come back. It felt hotter than the predicted record 104 degrees standing there on the Jamisons' front porch. The heat penetrated my skin and I reveled in its absoluteness, its power and authority. In a strange way, the furnace-like heat felt good to me. I let go of Tigger's leash and let her find relief in the nearby shade. The front door opened.

The girl standing before me wasn't the Katelyn Jamison I remembered bouncing around in her cheerleading uniform at West High. This young woman was sullen and tentative. Her onyx hair was parted down the middle. Her skin was much paler than I remembered. There were dark circles under her eyes. The large, black t-shirt she was wearing hung on her, disguising her pregnant belly, but making her arms and legs look like pencils. She wasn't wearing any make up and her pale blue eyes looked morose.

"I thought you'd give up and leave," Katelyn mumbled, still

standing in the doorway. "I don't really understand why you're here anyway," she said coolly.

And I thought we'd had a breakthrough.

Tigger approached, her claws clicking on the concrete front porch. She licked Katelyn's hand and I saw a reluctant smile pass across her faint pink lips.

"Aw, hi girl." She squatted down. "Is Tigger a girl?"

"Yep. Tigger's my best gal. Not exactly the most feminine name in the world, I know, but it works, with the stripes and all." I was rambling, shifting my weight and working hard to suppress the urge to wring my hands. I stuck my hands inside the pockets of my jeans and took a deep, audible breath, wishing I'd brought along Virginia Woolf.

"You're a sweetie pie," Katelyn cooed to Tigger, who licked her cheek in reply. "Oh thanks, sweet girl, you're so soft. I wish I could keep you, yes I do, that's right, girl."

Katelyn stood up again.

"So, really, why are you here?" She asked.

"Like I told you before, I thought you could use a friend." I didn't want to tell her Sister Dearborn had insisted I come. I knew that would make me sound trite and insincere.

"Just out of the blue, you want to be nice to the girl you've always thought was a perfect snob?" she snapped. "It's a little hard to believe."

I knew my answer to her question would mean the difference between Katelyn turning herself around and walking back inside her house and never talking to me again, and my succeeding in this battle of wills Sister Dearborn had started. I clapped my hands together to make myself stop wringing them and I stepped forward, reaching down to pet Tigg as I approached.

"Katelyn, I told you that I know how it feels to be alone and I meant it. I know how it feels to be on the outside looking in, watching others go on dates, to parties, out to dinner, and not be invited. You know, how you must be feeling now, because of the . . ."

I ran my fingers through my hair trying to go a different direction. "I mean, I practically received honors in 'being left behind at West.'"

Katelyn smiled. She appeared to be holding back laughter. So, naturally, I continued.

"Yeah, I was elected student body president of the lonely loser club. Maybe you've heard of it? The tryouts were pretty macabre. Be glad you missed them, though I'm sure you wanted to come, had you not been so busy being the most well-liked girl in school." I started to dance, doing a jig like a tap-dancer on stage tapping away maniacally for applause.

"Welcome to the 'lonely loser club,' that's L.L.C. for you and me!" I sang, standing there in Katelyn's doorway. I was off-key, of course. "The only place where doing something like this . . ." I pretended to trip and fall flat on my face in the lawn (what was I, crazy?) ". . . is okay!"

I looked up at Katelyn and inhaled the fresh scent of the grass under my chin. Tigger was running around me, putting her nose in my face, oblivious to the joke and thinking I needed help.

Katelyn threw her head back and clapped her hands together in a guffaw that appeared to be cathartic. Some pink color returned to her drawn face and she looked like the pretty Katelyn I had remembered.

"All right," Katelyn said, her hands in the air, trying to stifle her laughter. "You win. Come inside, please."

I thought about waving my fists in the air and shouting to myself "yes!" but felt like that would most certainly be inappropriate. Besides, once inside, what was I going to say next?

I forgot to call my mom and let her know where I was, so while I was leaving her a message on the phone, Katelyn sat on a stool at the polished granite island in her family's pristine kitchen doodling on a notepad. Everything shined around her, the stainless steel dishwasher, the scoured ceramic sinks, and the sparkling pots hanging above her on the sophisticated rack. Katelyn seemed a million miles away even though we were sitting just a few feet from each other. I could see she was drawing a stick family with her pencil, a dad, the tallest, with a cartoon bow tie, a mother with long, straight lead hair, and in between them a circular, smiling baby with ringlets on top of her head. In her dreamlike state, Katelyn drew hearts all around the little fantasy family. And then drawing the edges of the mother's mouth upward, she punctuated the two dimensional woman's smile to an even more jubilant expression. It struck me how everything must be going so terribly opposite the way Katelyn Jamison had dreamed her life would be. What had always seemed like an easy, safe, sure-thing dream was now as elusive and imaginary to her as Santa Claus.

When she noticed that I was finished, she quickly covered her sketch with her other hand.

"So what have you been up to this summer to amuse yourself?" she asked, still looking down and finishing her cloaked drawing.

"I went to Italy and France with my grandparents at the beginning of the summer. What a trip. It was, well, kind of life-changing for me." I moved a little closer and sat down on the stool next to her. She stopped drawing and shoved the notepad into the top drawer in the island and crumpled her paper and dropped it into the trash, ending a futile dream.

"Really, how so?" She asked, getting up and pulling two glasses out of the cupboard. As she turned, I noticed the little rounded shape of her belly, a life taking hold. The contrasting miracle of it all, and devastation of the circumstances for both Katelyn and the baby, touched my soul.

I explained to Katelyn all about my grandparents' strange notion of me as their little Renaissance beauty. She handed me a clear glass full of icy lemonade, and looked perplexed, remaining silent as she sipped her drink.

"Pathetic, isn't it? Like I was born into the wrong time or something. Anyway they took me to a gallery to see some of the art they were talking about. And, well, I do look like a lot of the women in those oil paintings." I continued, though Katelyn's lack of response made me nervous. Either I was losing her attention and potential trust completely or she was captivated.

"Put any of those women on TV today and people might be nothing but critical of them. Take *The Mona Lisa* for example, one of the most famous paintings in the world. *Da Vinci* certainly saw something striking about her. But could you picture her on the cover of *Vogue* today, or even hosting a news program? I think not."

"Maybe he didn't paint her because he thought she was gorgeous," Katelyn said thoughtfully. "I don't know, maybe he just found her memorable. He could've been in love with her or something, but for other reasons than physical beauty, more lasting reasons." Katelyn looked down at the hardwood floors. Her sadness went past tears, like a deep, dark cloud that never yields rain but hangs around long enough to turn into a tornado.

"So where's your mom?" I asked, trying to change the subject.

"She's at the store or something, I don't know. I don't care," answered Katelyn. She got up and walked to the living room. I took this as a signal for Tigger and me to leave. I gulped down the rest of my lemonade. Then, we followed behind her to the door. I felt let down. Our visit had been less than successful. I suddenly had the urge to run out of there as fast as my legs would carry me, confident that Tigg could keep up. We'd be a flash of fur and tennis shoes, a muss of red, frizzy hair and stripes. I forced myself to follow her at a normal pace.

Katelyn turned to me. The dark circles were a sharp contrast to her sky blue eyes. "You could come back tomorrow if you'd like. I mean, you could bring Tigger or something."

I couldn't believe it. Somehow, someway, I had entered into her dark, lonely world.

"Well, all right, that would be great!" I said while smiling large and wide. "Why don't we take Tigger to the park? I know she'd love that."

"I don't know about that. I don't really want to go anywhere." Katelyn looked down again, placing both hands on her belly. I was standing in the doorway and she was about to close it and lock it behind her.

I responded sprightly. "No problem. I'll just come by here in the afternoon again so you can see Tigger." My eyes subconsciously lingered on the little lump, the baby growing inside her, and I was sure she noticed. I felt rude and terrible. "No problem at all."

❧ ❧ ❧

I remember pretending it didn't matter that everyone I knew at West High was at prom that night except for me. I wished the minutes would pass in sped-up motion. My mom offered to take me to dinner that lonely night. I resisted for fear of coming across some members of my senior class dressed in pink satin or bejeweled in royal blue sequins. There would be a heavy corsage of stargazer lilies and carnations on their wrists, and their hair would be plastered to their heads in a do a hairdresser fashioned six hours before. How could they stand it? Enduring the heavy weight of the hair, the tightness of the bobby pins, the constricting feeling in the lungs from all that aerosol hairspray?

Truth was, I wanted my hair done in that bun as much as I'd

wanted anything in my life. I longed for the nervous feeling of a boy coming to pick me up. Would he think I was pretty? I wanted to worry about tripping in my high-heeled shoes. And I wished for the sickness in the pit of my stomach over the pending awkward moment at the end of the night that begged the question: to kiss or not to kiss.

I remember how I had pushed all these thoughts aside and turned off the light to my bedroom and wished the night away. That was when the doorbell rang.

There had been a high pitched, muffled chatter on the other side of my bedroom door that could only be Grams and my mom. They sounded a bit like two hens fighting over the right to roost in a very small hen house. Whatever happened to polite greetings?

"Knock-knock," Grams said, peeking her head inside my bedroom door. She had been wearing scarlet lipstick, a crimson silk shirt and fire engine red polyester pants. There was a chunky fake gold necklace around her neck and heavy gold earrings that made her lobes droop nearly to her shoulders.

"Just thought you could use some company, Avie." Grams had walked in and disapprovingly eyed the messy tapestry of magazines, books, and dirty clothes on my bedroom floor. "Why, it must be tough with everyone else at the P-R-O-M." Why she spelled out the last word was a mystery to me; after all, I learned to spell an awfully long time ago.

"Yeah, Grams, I know. It's pretty hard to forget where everybody else is tonight. But honestly, I could care less. It's just a big stupid party where people get drunk and vomit and do things they will later regret. No, thank you." I had opened up a book hoping Grams would get the signal that I didn't want to be bothered and kindly leave me alone.

I felt the mattress give way as she sat down next to me. I couldn't help gazing down at her two-tone crimson and white heels bedecking her swollen ankles and feet.

"Now honey-pie," she patted my leg. "Those boys don't know what they're missing. Why, anybody can see what a treasure you are. They can't recognize the beauty. They're only interested in tanned golden girls with thin thighs and large chests! You can't help it if you're not at all like that. Poor thing, you got a lot of your mom's looks, which I'm afraid came from Papa's side of the family. Unlucky, in that regard, I suppose."

I was starting to feel even more uncomfortable than before, a little queasy, even.

"If only Renaissance Art was a part of West High's curriculum." She clucked with her tongue.

"Grams, I know you mean well. Really, I do. And I guess I appreciate it. But I'd rather be left alone tonight. I'm fine. I'll survive, okay?" I put my hand on top of hers. Then, I saw her face brighten.

From Grams' point of view, she was a first-rate grandmother, caring, sweet, kind, helpful and wise. I'm certain she believed her brutally honest observations helped me, instead of sending me further into despair. I knew she loved me and didn't mean to hurt me. There was no guile to her insults. Still, this knowledge never took the sting away. No one ever wants to hear about their faults. Most of us are painfully aware of them already.

It was a tradition my grandmother passed down to my mother, relentlessly, and hence, to me. Insults in the name of self-improvement; a cruel family heirloom. The problem was the method never achieved the goal. It further scarred the person and backed her deeper into her shell of rejection. The things my mother said to me were painful echoes of the heated exchanges I'd witnessed between Grams and Mom all my life. I wondered when the destructive pendulum would stop swinging.

When I returned home from Katelyn's house, Mom and I were polite to one another. We went through cycles like this, cool politeness, building annoyances, and all-out fighting. This beginning phase of the cycle was oddly my least favorite because the looming pain was sure to come in the horizon. I moved around her, fixing my own dinner saying "Excuse me," and "Would you mind handing me the cheddar cheese and salsa, please?" She was on another crazy diet, abstaining from what I was eating, trying to lose those ten pounds she had complained about since the day I was born. Mom was chopping some strange concoction in the blender when I stuck my plate of nachos into the microwave. In between her grinding, ice crushing, and blending the unappetizingly green mixture, I heard the phone ring and jumped on it.

"Hello?" Mom turned on the blender again. I pantomimed wildly for her to stop.

"I'm sorry, hi, who's this?" I said into the receiver.

"Avery. It's Barclay." His voice sounded as toneless as a computer greeting.

"Hey Barc. What's wrong?"

"It's my mom. She's succeeded this time." He sounded distressingly calm.

"What happened?" I stood to my feet and wanted to jump out of my skin.

He was silent. I couldn't tell if he was being distant or pushing back a waterfall of tears.

"I'll be right over," I said.

I threw down the phone, told my mom I was going to Barclay's and I'd call her later. I ignored her protests to know more. I ran up I Street as fast as my legs would carry me.

There were sirens glowing like visual panic outside of Barclay's brown house. Police cars were parked at odd angles on the street, and there was an ambulance with the back doors open wide. A fire truck screamed as it pulled up with its bright flashes of red, yellow and white light. It was like a nightmare. Finally, I spotted another long, white vehicle that had written on the side "County Coroner."

Two men wearing gloves wheeled a body on a stretcher zipped up in a black bag out the front door. I gasped and thought I might throw up. The image of his quiet, distant mother with the dark crescents under her eyes kept flashing through my mind. How could she be dead? I just saw her briefly yesterday. She had lived on my street all of my life, a silent shadow in the background, and a constant worry for her son.

I found Barclay inside talking with the police. He was talking stiffly with his hands. He jerked his wavy hair out of his face. I saw the policeman put his hand on Barclay's slumped shoulder.

I heard my lifelong friend tell the policeman as I walked closer, "It's going to be okay. I'm a survivor by nature. This won't destroy me."

With all my heart, I wished that I could've believed him.

My chin began to quiver and my eyes welled up with tears when I saw Barclay. The strong, in-control expression he held for the policeman quickly melted when he saw me. I put my arms out toward him and we embraced. It was like I was holding him up. I felt his weight leaning on me. I could feel his body heaving with the magnitude of his sadness.

The policeman turned the other way, averting his eyes from us.

"How could she leave me like this, Avery?" he asked between choking sobs. "She has her problems, I mean, she had her problems. But she was my mother! Mothers can't bail! How could she? I can't believe she's gone . . ."

I held Barclay there for a long time. Then, we sat on the front lawn while the police finished up their investigation. Yellow crime scene tape wrapped around his house giving it a menacing appearance. Police investigators walked in and out carrying plastic bags full of evidence. Passersby slowed down in their cars to have a look. A few neighbors gathered on the outskirts of his yard wearing concerned expressions and talking softly to one another. Barclay sat on the grass next to me with his knees propped up and his head between them studying the ground, his hair flopped over in one big heap. Every now and then his shoulders would heave again and he'd press his hands up against his face, trying to regain composure that wouldn't come.

"Barclay, I'm so sorry for your loss. It's hard to find the appropriate words to say to you right now, other than I'm sorry. And it's important to me that you know I'm not going anywhere. I'm here for you."

"Thanks," he said weakly.

I put my hand on his shoulder and he leaned over and embraced me. He buried his head on my shoulder and we rocked there for a while.

"Your mother loved you, Barc. She was just very ill. I'm sure she didn't even know what she was doing." Nothing I could've said felt like it was enough.

"Loved me? How can you be so sure?" He cried. "If she loved me she would've stuck it out. You stick it out when you love someone."

"I'm afraid it's not that simple. You know how long she's struggled with this. She finally lost her battle with a very serious disease."

Barclay put his head between his legs again. He cried so hard a stream of saliva dripped from his mouth onto the ground. It was excruciating seeing my dear friend in so much pain.

"It's not always going to hurt this bad, Barc. Time will heal. That's what Papa always tells me. This too shall pass."

I took his hand in mine and squeezed firmly. We stayed there in the yard until the sun went down and all the investigators left. That night, Barclay slept on the monster couch at my house. My mom didn't say one word in protest. I fixed him some graham crackers and milk, but he wouldn't even touch them. Finally, at about 2:00 a.m., sleep overcame him. I went into my room, pulled up the covers, and patted the bed for Tigger to jump up and warm my feet, which she obliged.

Barclay had a long road of healing ahead of him. I was completely exhausted emotionally and physically. I felt like a lemon that had been squeezed thoroughly with not a drop of juice left. My head was pounding with a massive headache, perhaps the beginnings of a migraine.

Still, I pulled out the little post card and my notepad and began to write.

> *Dear Lucrezia,*
>
> *My best friend's mom killed herself. Barclay found her lying on the floor of her bedroom next to an empty bottle of pills. She kept down a lethal dose of something long enough to kill her. She'd been dead for several hours before Barclay went looking for her. It wasn't uncommon for her to spend days at a time in bed, not even coming out to see the son she loved. I have a mixture of pity and hatred for his mom. I hate her for what she did to Barclay. I despise her for making a young man constantly worry so much about his mother when he should be out being careless and making his own mistakes.*
>
> *I feel sorry for her, too. After all, she was very sick. Maybe we all could've done more to have helped her.*
>
> *It's my job now to try and help Barclay through this . . .*
> *More later,*
> *Avery*

6

Barclay and I sat on the edge of the dirt road that wound up Lamb's Canyon. This was our favorite spot. We didn't like Park City or Deer Valley as much. Though beautiful, those places were just too touristy for both of us. Lamb's Canyon is a sleepy place tucked between Salt Lake City and the Park City resorts. I suppose it's a pit stop for most people. The mountain has too steep an incline to become a pristine destination. But for Barclay and me, it was a haven.

The canyon's sharp angle had its advantages, allowing it to be more isolated than most. Only a few log cabin homes dotted the extreme mountainside. Scalloped, green leaves on the aspen trees rustled in the wind. God's landscaping grew lush and green above the rustic, rocky road, thick like a canopy. Sunlight barely filtered through, like angels singing. We heard the faint whisper of a small mountain stream taking its time winding downhill.

While I sat there with Barclay, we made eye contact with an elk that stood 15 feet from us. We knew she would come no closer. Two chipmunks scampered by near our feet. Robins overhead swooped and circled singing their chirpy songs, seemingly without a care in the world. I squeezed Barclay's hand and prayed for the right words to come to me.

If one's soul could wear a sling, Barclay's would've been heavily bandaged.

I let my sandals skim the top of the dirt where we sat. I wished I could take his pain away.

He was leaning on me as we sat there resting our elbows on our knees in the rich earth by the little road. I could hear his slow and purposeful breathing. I knew that every single moment was painful. Barclay was suffering, just trying to get through the days since his mom's funeral. Nearly the whole neighborhood showed up to pay respects, like a helping hand extended a little too late. I put my arm around him and squeezed his shoulder. We sat there a long time before he spoke.

"Avery? Can I tell you something?" His voice sounded like someone who wasn't speaking his native tongue, thinking through every word before he said it.

"Sure, Barc, anything."

Barclay said, "I can't believe how I'm feeling right now. I've got to get this off my chest. A part of me is relieved. Relieved that she finally did it." His voice sounded fragile now, like a dam about to burst open. "I mean, all my life she has threatened to do it and it's always terrified me. She even tried a couple of times. I used to be plagued by, 'what if?' Now the worst has happened. In a strange way, I don't have to worry about it happening anymore. I must be really messed up."

Barclay let his head drop while still resting his elbows on his knees. He was monitoring a tiny colony of ants below.

"Barclay, I'm sure it's completely normal to feel that way," I said, not even believing my own words. "You are feeling intense grief, Barc, and everybody experiences it differently. Don't berate yourself for your feelings. Your feelings are valid. I'm sure there's no surefire formula to getting over something as tragic as this. You have to find your own way."

He reached over and put his arms around me and put his head on my shoulder. He was crying big fat tears that soaked my t-shirt. I looked up at the Aspen trees standing so tall and proud, their leaves flickering in the summer wind. I said a little prayer in my heart that Heavenly Father would comfort Barclay and help me be the friend that he needed.

"I miss her so much, Ave. I can't believe she's gone." He sobbed. "Really gone. I want her to be home waiting for me when I get home later. I didn't need her to do much for me, but just knowing she was there was still a comfort. I know she loved me, Avie. Despite everything she couldn't do, I always knew she loved me more than anything."

I looked up into his eyes, bloodshot and full of tears. I saw intense anguish and two replicas of my own empathetic expression reflected in his dark pupils.

"That's a gift you'll have forever, Barclay, the love she had for you. No one can ever take that away. You are blessed in that way, Barc. Despite how it ended, there were still blessings." I took his face in my hands and kissed him on his stubbly cheek. "I love you, friend."

"I love you, too," he said, so easily. He seemed to brighten a bit then. We interlaced the fingers of our hands and watched a mother duck slip into the green stream below in the distance. Six little dots of yellow fuzz plopped in dutifully behind her.

***

The summer leaves transformed into hues of pale yellow, earth and fire. There was electricity in the air, a freshness brought in by the early fall chill. It was beckoning, expectant and alive. The Hawthorne trees in the valley sprouted their jubilant red berries and patches along the highway had rows of orange and yellow pumpkins. The tree trunks were dark and brooding, the outline of their branches intricately reaching to the sky.

People on the streets in the Avenues were wearing their cotton sweaters, boots and rain slickers. Kids were sporting their new school clothes, autumn stripes on rugby shirts layered over t-shirts and khakis. Little girls walking to school were bedecked with pleated skirts and tights with stripes all colors of the rainbow on their skinny, knobby knees. The kids proudly carried their new backpacks bulging with new pencils and plastic rulers in their zippered pockets.

I began my classes at the U, the bulk of them were on Mondays, Wednesdays, and Fridays, beginning with sociology first thing in the mornings and ending with English Lit in the afternoons. I usually dressed for comfort, wearing a t-shirt with a sweatshirt over it or tied at my waist, and mismatched drawstring sweat pants. I donned a baseball cap and carried my books in the backpack I slung lazily over one shoulder, carrying my text books, but also, my friends. Most days I went to and from class without talking or even making eye contact with another living soul.

❦

After all of his waffling, he finally did it. Barclay left for MIT. Their classes began later than ours at the U. Still, he had already missed the first couple of weeks. He dropped some of his classes, opting for a light load to give him time to catch up. I suppose that his mom's untimely death forced a new kind of courage on him. "I've gotta get out of here, Avery," he said. "I've got to go get going and just do this. You know?" His dad, who I'd hardly ever seen, sold the brown house on I Street. Barclay packed his things.

The day Barclay left for school, I wept. I drove him to the airport. The new security restrictions made painful good-byes so abbreviated, so unfinished. That hot afternoon at the end of summer, I pulled up my clunky car to the Delta skycap area. I helped Barclay pull two heavy, cumbersome leather duffle bags out of my trunk. The airport was a bustle with summer travelers returning home and other students headed to universities. It was chaotic and my heart was throbbing inside my chest.

Barclay and I looked at one another and I grabbed a hold of his one free hand. We stood together there, amidst the chaos, and hugged for a long time. We didn't say anything. When I pulled away, I could see that he was crying, too. A part of me wanted to crawl inside his large carry-on and go with him. As soon as he was out of sight, I felt a pang like I did each time I finished reading *Catcher in the Rye,* only stronger.

I was visiting Katelyn every afternoon after class now. Sometimes I'd bring her thick and greasy hot dogs from the cafeteria from the union, trying to satisfy her biggest craving. She savored those disgusting ones that have been rolling on little warmers for heaven only knows how long. I found the strange cravings of pregnancy amusing.

It turns out we had a lot more in common than ever seemed plausible. She loved to read, too, and longed to travel to far-off places. Katelyn lived for the stories I told her about Florence. I embellished them a little, anything to brighten her days during this difficult time. She too, had a tough relationship with her mother, though they seemed like best friends by all outward appearances. You never would've known they struggled. Sometimes people are like those ducks Barclay and I saw in the stream at Lamb's Canyon, calm and serene on the surface and fighting with all their might to stay afloat beneath the surface.

"Ah—there she goes again, the baby kicked! Want to feel her?" Katelyn's eyes were bright, her mouth turned up at the ends, as she leaned back on a pile of fluffy pillows edged in ruffles in the living room.

I put my hand on her tight belly, feeling more than a little uncomfortable. But I was surprised at the force of the little punch underneath her cotton maternity blouse and taut skin. I was touching a miracle, maybe a misplaced one, but still. There was such strength in that little person in there already.

"Wow, that's amazing! What does it feel like when she does that to you?"

Katelyn sloppily gnawed on the hot dog I'd brought her. It was plump and topped generously with relish, catsup and mustard. She licked her fingers in between bites.

Her face had a healthy glow. Her pale cheeks were slightly pink and the darkness underneath her eyes was lighter than I'd seen in months. She rested her legs on the polished mahogany coffee table, leaning all the way back on the couch. Her belly protruded to a new height in this position.

"First it felt like butterflies in my stomach, little flutters." She said knowingly, caressing her belly. "Then, I felt definite movement, little brushes inside my belly. And finally now, whoa, major kicks! It's really powerful. She can sure wield a blow."

"Does it hurt when she wallops you?"

"Oh no. Just pressure. It's funny though, whenever we're in the mall, the grocery store, whatever we're doing, when she kicks I want to shout, 'Wow! Did anyone else notice that? My daughter just kicked me with her strong legs!'" Katelyn was smiling. It struck me then how much she looked like a little girl sitting and grinning, a little girl who was forced to find maturity beyond her years. Her smile quickly disappeared. "Of course I'd never shout like that. My mom is so mortified already. I think she secretly hates me to go anywhere with her. I'm her poster child for bad decisions, I guess. 'The Mistake.'" She sat up and looked out the window at some other, imaginary life, the life that could've been.

"The only difference is that your mistake is obvious to everyone right now. Everyone else's foul-ups are often hidden, not obvious at first glance. But we all make mistakes." I scratched Tigger's bent ear as I talked to Katelyn. "That's why we're here, right? To learn from them and try to do better?"

Katelyn took the last bite of hot dog and enjoyed it like a dieter who has been deprived for months, now savoring the last piece of chocolate cake. "My mom actually makes me wear these big ol' dark t-shirts to cover up. I want to wear those cute fitted and tight belly shirts. I think they look so cute and they really are the style now, 'no more muumuus!'" We both laughed. "Pregnancy is a beautiful shape," she continued. "Too bad I have to remain camouflaged. I mean, everyone and their dog already knows."

"Now that's true!" I rose to my feet and slapped my thighs, signaling Tigg to jump up. "Everyone and their dog—that's us!" Tigger and I danced like a clumsy Fred Astaire and Ginger Rogers. Anything to make Katelyn laugh.

∗∗∗

Katelyn was certain that her baby was going to be a girl. Her parents wouldn't spring for the extra cost of an ultrasound, reasoning that Katelyn knowing the sex of her baby might make her too attached, that it might make it impossible for her to give the baby up.

A kind woman from LDS Social Services had already visited three times at Katelyn's parents' request. She left pamphlets of happy, attractive fathers and mothers with a little girl in ponytails sitting in between their loving arms. On the front the pamphlets read: "You're not giving her up, you are giving her more."

We walked into Katelyn's pale pink room with white wainscoting. Her trashcan was littered with these pamphlets, torn and crumpled. Her room smelled faintly of a flowery perfume. I noticed only one pamphlet remained intact on her nightstand under an empty soda can. I craned my neck to read the title, "Open Adoption: A Loving Option."

Katelyn plopped down on her bed with surprising agility given her pregnant girth. I looked up above her mirrored closet doors. Photos of her and her high school friends were a mosaic of wallpaper. All the pictures were of before. There was Katelyn in the middle of a group of pretty girlfriends, smiling like she didn't have a care in the world. There was another of her by herself, hands in the air, striking a model's pose. There were other pictures of her with her brothers, taken in the manicured back yard, and a few in her red and black cheerleading uniform. There was a snapshot at the very top of Katelyn smiling with her arms around her mother.

Looking at the wall of pictures, you'd think Katelyn was full of her self, conceited. I was beginning to realize that, in fact, the opposite was true. Often the ones who work so hard to show that they belong have the most fragile self-esteem of all.

"I'm going to name her Payton." Katelyn broke the silence. "After my Grandma and Grandpa Payton. They love me no matter what, that's what Grandma Payton always says. I think they're the only ones who support my wanting to keep this baby. At least, they say they'll support whatever decision I make."

I crossed my legs on the floor, leaning back with my hands behind my head resting on the plush, beige carpet.

"How will you be able to care for her?" I asked. "I mean, I bet it will be so hard."

"How can I not care for her? She's my daughter. I'll find a way." There was ferocity in Katelyn's face. I had crossed a line.

I sat back up. "I'm sorry. I didn't mean to imply that you couldn't—"

"She belongs with me. That's all there is to it. I won't give her up. I can't give her up." Katelyn's eyes were welling up with tears. She hugged one of her rose-colored pillows close to her and the baby.

"What do your parents say?" I asked.

"They say that there are so many loving couples out there who don't have children and could provide a wonderful, complete home for her. They always say, 'As much as you want to, you can't possibly give her all that she needs.'" Katelyn's face was full of worry. "Maybe I could give her all she needs if I had supportive parents. It's just like their way or the highway. When they get together on something, there's no talking any sense into them, no way to reason at all. I feel trapped."

I felt uneasy, like I was walking into water that was slowly edging up and before I knew it, I would be in over my head.

She looked up at me. "Maybe Logan will come back to his senses. I know he still loves me, I just know it. He said he would love me forever. That's why it didn't feel so wrong when it happened. I thought our love for each other made it okay." Katelyn was studying her feet. "Maybe it will be okay. We could be a family. It could happen."

"Where is he in all of this?" I asked with bitterness.

"He ducked out. He wrote me a long letter explaining he was not ready for marriage. He also explained that he and his parents agreed the best option for everyone is adoption. 'Option,' he put it just like that, as if the decision were as simple as choosing a university, just weigh all the pros and cons and pick the side with the most positives. It's so much more complicated than that. Well, the love in my heart for this child just cannot be measured or tallied." She clapped her hands together and pointed forward. "It was just so easy for him to hit the road, so to speak. He's not attached."

She rubbed her belly lovingly and continued speaking. "What no one tells you is that most women fall in love with their babies immediately in the womb, right from the minute they discover they are pregnant, even if you didn't want the baby at first."

"It must've been devastating when you found out you were pregnant." I offered.

"It was, it was." She cringed and shook her head. "I never dreamed it could really happen. I didn't know what to do. I'd never been so down in the dumps and confused."

Now, I felt like I was definitely under the water, my head leaning back trying to get the last bit of precious oxygen.

"Well, Katelyn." I stood up slowly. Tigger jumped up beside me. "I want you to know you can count on me. I don't know what I can do, but I'm here and I want to help, any way that I can. Just know I'm here."

"What would you do, Avery?" She edged up on the bed and sounded desperate. "If you were in my shoes, what choice would you make?" Her eyes pled with me to confirm that she was making the right decision.

"It's so tough to say. At the risk of sounding corny, I don't know much about babies. I can't understand how you're feeling. But I know how much I love this mutt here." I ran my hand down Tigg's soft fur. "I bet the love I feel for her is only a fraction, minuscule, compared to how you feel about your baby."

Katelyn nodded her head slowly.

"With all that love that you have for her, I'm sure you will make the right decision. I know you will, Katelyn. I can't believe I'm going to say this, but, don't discount what your parents have to say. I'm not saying they're right." I put my hands up in defense. "But they care about you, just like you care for that life growing inside of you. That was you once remember. Hard to imagine sometimes, I'm sure. I'm sure your mom sat and rubbed her stomach just like you are now. I'm positive she worried and felt instant, unconditional love for you. She probably longed to hold you, like you do your own baby. Just try to listen to her. Take from her whatever advice you can."

I had never thought about it this way. I surprised myself with my wisdom. Then, the image of my own mother, pregnant with me, formed in my mind, and dissolved again quickly.

"There are no good options. I feel like I'm sinking, Avery; sinking, sinking, sinking."

"What about that one?" I asked her, pointing to the pamphlet on her nightstand. "Open adoption sounds nice. You'd still get to see your daughter, right? But not have all the burden of caring for her."

"It wouldn't be a burden!" Katelyn shrieked, her eyes wild.

"Sorry, sorry. That's not what I meant." Tigger squeaked with empathy. I scratched her downy soft chin. I was afraid I was losing Katelyn's trust and that she was beginning to see me as the enemy. I was touching her Achilles Heel.

"How does open adoption work, exactly?" I asked.

Katelyn looked down and rubbed her belly longingly. "It's still giving her up." She glanced back up at me, the dark circles even more pronounced from that vantage point. "But I guess I'd get to visit her. And, they'd send me letters and pictures of her all the time."

"So, essentially, you could still follow your dreams and have your baby in your life. Plus, two loving parents who you chose just for her would raise her. You could hand pick them according to what you think would be best for her, a mother and father who'd take care of her like you would if you could. It would be a win-win situation."

"There's no winning here, Avery," Katelyn said with disdain. "It's not a football game. Besides, I hate them already. Some lucky, happy couple who did everything right in life and now they want to take my baby away from me."

"Sorry. I'm just not saying what you want to hear today, am I? I'm sorry."

"I know you're just trying to help."

I held Tigger's leash in my hand and walked toward the front door.

"Avery?"

I turned back to Katelyn.

"Yeah?"

"You're a good friend."

"I am?"

"Yeah. You really are," she continued. "Thanks. I'll think about what you said."

I smiled warmly. No one had ever said anything like that to me before, no one like Katelyn. Tigg reached up and licked my hands.

As I walked out of Katelyn's fancy door, the one that had once been so daunting, I thought about how miraculous life is.

Dear Lucrezia,

I'm making great progress with my friend. In fact, I don't think I've ever had a friend, besides Barclay, who I've liked this much. I'm worried about her. She wants to keep this baby. I don't know how she'd manage it. Her parents are bent on her giving the baby up for adoption. Her ex-boyfriend, Logan, is as far out of the picture as possible. All that his parents offered was financial help with her medical bills. I wish I had the right answers for Katelyn.

I got a letter from Barclay today. He sounds really sad there at MIT. Moving away didn't help heal his broken heart. He's still as distraught and troubled by his mother's death as the day it happened, maybe even more so now. I guess he never realized just how much he'd miss her.

Barclay says he's doing well with his studies, though he misses me. He decided to major in aerospace aeronautical. I miss him too, more than I thought I would. I wish I could run up and ruffle his shaggy hair, too. I'm beginning to wonder if my feelings for Barclay are stronger than I realized before he left. I'd never tell anyone this, but I can't help but think about it.

As for my mom, well, I'm beginning to think that in her mind, she really thinks she's helping me when she says those mean things. I'm sure no new parent looks down at her infant and says, "Gee, I hope I can really screw up your life." I want to try harder to forgive my mother and to find harmony.

I don't know if I can ever forgive my dad, though. We'll see.

With Love,
Avery

7

The sun was high in the bright blue autumn sky. There was a chill in the air. The trees had lost most of their leaves and lay scattered around Katelyn and me in colorful piles, with their edges curling up.

I was enjoying my first semester at the U. I found the intensity of the classes an exhilarating change from high school, along with the anonymity the large lecture halls provided. I would slip in at the beginning and make a beeline for the exit once the professor finished. There were no more impenetrable cliques, no more long lunch hours where social standing was clearly defined by what group you sat with. The mix of people on campus was refreshing. There were granola types wearing earthy looking sandals and sporting uncombed hair, sitting near preppy, sorority types with thin bows in their loosely tied up hair.

There was more diversity in my average lecture hall than in the entire enrollment at West. People with skin the color of mocha, the *crème de caramel* I had seen in Italy, or as black as the buttons on my favorite sweater, dotted the room. There were usually a few older students with flecks of silver in their hair or around their temples, sitting near the front, seemingly drinking in every single word the professor spoke.

I loved walking comfortably alone on campus with my backpack slung over my shoulder. Lots of people strolled by in solitude, so I didn't stand out. I'd amble past the fountains to the student union for a snack, my battered copy of *Mrs. Dalloway* and *Lucrezia* keeping me company along the way. I aced my midterms. College worked well with my natural proclivity to be inconspicuous, and fed my deep hunger for knowledge.

At night the temperature froze into an icy promise of the winter to come. Thanksgiving was just around the corner.

It was chilly and brisk at the park. Katelyn wore her father's brown wool sweater that had corduroy patches on the elbows. She draped it across her blossoming belly and let the long sleeves fall over her hands. She was eight months along and carried a perfect, tight ball in front of her. The way she was sitting on the grassy hill made her look like she could go into labor at any moment. A wave of panic consumed me in the peaceful setting.

I sat next to Katelyn after a walk with Tigg around the jogging track in the park. Tigger seemed antsy on the walk. She was not used to Katelyn's slower pace, made tenuous because she felt the pull of ligaments around her hips and had the uneasy feeling she might collapse.

It took some convincing for Katelyn to slow down and take it easy. At least she let me carry her backpack for her. "Don't slow up on account of me," she said, gasping for breath. Katelyn seemed to be trying to prove she could do everything that she could before she was pregnant, as if that would somehow make her life more normal. Denial? Either way, from what I'd read, too much strenuous exercise at this late stage of her pregnancy could throw her into early labor. It was clear that Katelyn loved this baby dearly but was already having trouble coping. Yet, how could she? She really couldn't even care for herself, let alone, someone else.

"Any luck yet?" I asked her.

"Nah. They're all too perfect, if that makes any sense," she told me.

Katelyn pulled out a stack of letters and photos from a large envelope in her backpack. It was a pile of smiling faces, white teeth, freshly pressed blouses and button downs, hands clasped together, arms around each other, hopeful shining eyes: her baby's potential parents.

"Like this one, the Pratts. Both graduated at the top of their classes at BYU. He in business, she in elementary ed. Married in the temple eight years ago, she's the Relief Society President. He's the Elders Quorum Pres. Look at them. If you looked up 'perfect couple' in the dictionary, the Pratts would be pictured there."

They did look squeaky clean in the photo wearing their matching white cotton shirts and khaki pants embracing each other in front of a waterfall.

"I mean listen to their 'faults.'" Katelyn rustled the neatly typed form in her hands. "David: works too hard and cares too much about his family. Lee Ann: does too much for others. Those are bad things? Please."

"I don't get it," I told her. "Don't you want someone like the Pratts raising your baby?"

"Nah, they're not right. Sure, I want someone better than me, but not someone from a different planet. I need to see that they're real, too."

Katelyn fingered through the stack of freshly coiffed couples. "Nope, nope, nope. They're all wrong for her. Look at these two: they wrote 'NONE' in the blank for faults. Now how is that possible? No faults at all? How is that possible?"

Katelyn shook her head.

"What about them?" I asked her. I pointed to a picture that had dropped out of the stack and lay on the green grass in front of us. It was a close-up snapshot of a jubilant man and woman laughing in each other's arms on the beach somewhere. They weren't posed like people in the other professional photos in the pile. The woman's blond hair was frizzy and she was laughing so hard you could almost see her tonsils. Her husband had a little stubble on his chin and his teeth were crooked. He had a pronounced overbite, noticeable because of his wide, happy grin.

"Oh, them. I hadn't really thought about them. The Carters?"

"They look happy, and not so perfect," I offered.

"Says here the photo was taken on a secluded beach in Mexico that's off the beaten path, their favorite vacation spot, far away from the typical tourist jaunts. They went there on their honeymoon and they go back each year for their anniversary," she said. "Hmm. Nice."

"What about their 'faults?'" I inquired.

Katelyn searched through her stack to find their form. "Ah, let's see now. 'Buddy: sleeps too much, cranky when he wakes up. Hates vegetables. Has a weakness for candy bars. Mallory: annoyed with Buddy's sleeping late and cranky from his crankiness. Perpetually, irreversibly late—comes from a long line of people who can't get anywhere on time.'"

Katelyn continued, "Buddy added an arrow pointing to more. 'Oh, and I'm annoyed that Mallory is always late.'" Katelyn looked up at me and smiled. "So they're not morning people, and not punctual," she shrugged her shoulders. "I like them. They're honest."

Tigger was lounging in between us. Katelyn reached over and scratched her head with her dainty fingers. Tigger seemed to love the attention. Then, unexpectedly, she let out a small puff of a bark in warning, just enough to fluff up the sides of her mouth where her whiskers were. She cocked a crooked ear.

Then we saw the object of Tigger's concern. A slender boy with dark hair and strong features walked on the rocks along the side of the stream. He was balancing, wearing dirty, white tennis shoes. A younger boy who looked quite similar to him followed not far behind. Where was their mother?

The older boy looked up at us as he approached but didn't smile. He was working at something below the shallow water, easing it out. He walked toward us carrying his prize, a large rock that was nearly rectangular in shape, with brown fungus on the bottom and pale green fungus on top that shimmered in the sunlight. He gently placed it at our feet, and then dutifully went back to the water to retrieve another. The second was small, pale, round, and smooth. It clicked when it hit the other rock, adding to the offering at our feet. The boy continued collecting rocks of all shapes and sizes from the brook until there was a good-sized pile in front of Katelyn, Tigger and me. I was fascinated watching him and a little intrigued about his motives. Katelyn and I studied him in silence. Each time he brought up a new rock Tigg would cock her head to the side in a question mark.

"What's your name?" I asked as he came closer, this time with a jagged, white rock.

"Tuck. That's short for Tucker." He dropped the rock with a clank on top of the others.

"How old are you, Tuck?" I asked.

"I'm eight," he said, still studying the rocks.

Katelyn arched her back and squirmed, trying to get comfortable on the hard ground. She asked, "Where did your brother go?"

"He's probably up at the play ground." Tuck seemed completely unconcerned about his younger brother. I got the sense that they were used to spending many hours here alone.

"And your mom? Where's she?" I asked.

"At our apartment, just across the street." Tuck shrugged his shoulders. "She might walk over in a little while." Tuck dug through to the bottom of the pile and picked up the first rock he had brought over and held it in his hands.

"See? This one looks like a school bus," he said, turning it over for us to inspect. He put the rock down and picked up another. "This one looks like a face." He showed us the two top indentations on its flat surface, one small bulge in the middle, and a faint little line underneath that looked like a mouth. The rocks were his treasures.

He pulled out a smashed sandwich that was in a Ziploc bag in his pocket, tossing it to the ground like he was *Monet* too engrossed in a watercolor for a bothersome necessity like food.

"It does look like a bus, Tuck," I said. "You're quite creative."

Katelyn and I continued talking as we watched him. He had a knowing grin on his face while he continued working on the rock pile.

I turned to speak to Katelyn. "How will you know when it's time?"

"The doctors say I'll just know. I can already feel pressure a little lower, like the baby has dropped. But I still feel great and can really do everything I did before. No problem. I'm dreading the labor part. I hear it's excruciating."

"You scared?" I tore a leaf in half and let it fall to the ground.

"Terrified."

"I would be, too, Katelyn. No doubt about that."

"Will you be there?" Katelyn jolted forward to attention. "In the birthing room, Avery? I know it's a lot to ask. But you are the truest friend I think I've ever had, even though I've only really gotten to know you the past few months. Everybody else has forgotten about me, all my 'best friends.' They're pretty much off doing their own things now, too busy to worry about their pregnant 'loser' friend. But you, Avery, you come to see me every single day. I want you to be there."

I felt sweat accumulating in my arm pits and hoped it wasn't going to be obvious how nervous and uncomfortable I was, though very flattered, too.

"What about your mom, Katelyn? I'm sure she'll want to be the one to help you."

"No. She can be in there, that's fine. I'm sure she'll insist. But I want you to be my coach. You know, help me through. Like Coach Jackson at West, encouraging me along the way. Got it?" Katelyn sounded more like she was talking about a cheerleading competition than the birth of her child. I was beginning to wonder if she truly realized the gravity of the situation or how huge of a life decision this was going to be. "We can practice and everything," she continued, with perkiness in her voice. "That Lamaze class, or whatever they call it. Maybe it will be fun."

"I don't know, Katelyn. I mean, I'm so honored you would ask me. It just seems like such a big thing. What do I know about babies? Zilch." I crossed my legs and wrung my hands.

"Like I said, I'm sure someone can teach you everything you need to know. Please, Avery. It would mean so much to me. Don't give up on me now." Her tone was very close to a whine. "Avery? Please?

"All right. How can I say no? I'll be there to help you. You can count on me. I just hope I don't faint."

"Do you faint when you see blood?"

"No, no. At least I don't think I do. Let's hope not. And hey, babies are born every day, right? No biggie. Piece of cake." My voice was trembling.

"You are truly the greatest, Avery! You really are!" She reached over her bulging belly and hugged me around the shoulders. "What would I ever do without you? Why God sent me you, I may never know. But I'm grateful." We sat there for a long while. For the first time that I can remember, I was at a complete loss for words. I ruffled Tigg's ears and hugged her close around the neck for comfort.

Just then Tucker turned to leave. His shorts were completely muddy and his white t-shirt was soaked.

"Bye, Tucker," I called. "It sure was nice meeting you!"

He turned around and took several steps closer to me, gingerly balancing on the smooth stones beneath him. Tucker's mouth was open but his lips were closed and pressed down to suppress a grin. He leaned toward me, dripping stream water on my toes.

"I think you're pretty," he said in a soft voice. He turned and clumsily ran through the water, down the brook, and far out of sight.

My face felt warm. Then, I felt a grin stretch across my face. This was another milestone. I'd never had a complete stranger give me such a nice compliment. Me? Pretty? They say that kids don't lie.

❧❧❧

I put off dinner with my dad as long as possible. Finally, I responded to his phone calls and constant barrage of messages. He was picking me up in ten minutes. I stood there looking at my reflection in my bedroom mirror, combing my thin, wavy hair. What was he going to say? He said he had something very important to discuss. He wanted to "clear the air." What could possibly excuse leaving your family for a new one? What could ever fix that?

I smoothed on some pink lip-gloss and pressed my lips together. Nothing I'd tried on seemed right. There was a pile of clothes on my bed. I settled on an old stand-by, a white, ruffled button down that I didn't have time to iron and black, low rise, boot-cut pants. I looked classic, presentable and put together. Tigg was lying at my side with her snout resting on my carpet. She rested with her back toward me and her nose and ears pointed out, as if she was standing sentinel on a ship called "Avery's Life." I wished Tigger could come with me tonight. Or better yet, I longed to put on my pajamas and crawl into bed, and not go at all.

The doorbell rang.

I grabbed my favorite long gray wool sweater that tied at my waist. I turned for one last check in the mirror and noticed I was twirling a lock of my red hair with my index finger. I forced my hand down, fixed my hair and said a little prayer that I would calm down and make it through this difficult night.

Through the thin, wooden door of my bedroom, I could hear my parents' forced politeness. I knew I had to get down there as quickly as possible. The longer they spoke, the more likelihood there was for harsh words. How could these two people ever have been so much in love?

I sprayed a little perfume on my neck and checked my makeup in the mirror. I remembered when I had found an old wedding picture, still framed, underneath my mom's bed one day when she was at work. While I knew I shouldn't have been snooping through her things, sometimes I just couldn't help it. In the old photograph, she looked so young and happy. Her white skin was smooth and clear. Her blue eyes were bright and shining. Mom's brown hair was curled and she wore a white flower on the right side tucked behind her ear. Her white, satin wedding dress was simple and elegant, fitted perfectly to her trim frame. My dad looked like he was fresh off his mission. His grin was so big in the photo it looked like the tips of his mouth nearly touched his side burns. They hugged each other closely, like they couldn't get close enough. The light gray majesty of the Salt Lake Temple shined behind them. The picture couldn't have appeared more perfect.

My legs carried me downstairs to the two of them standing there in the doorway.

"Hey, there's my girl! You look lovely," Dad said. "Got some lotion there you're rubbing in?" He gestured toward my hands. I looked down, nervously, and planted my hands at my sides.

"No, no. Where're we going?" I asked.

"Sky's the limit. You decide, Avery. Anywhere you want to go is just great with me." Dad's hair was slicked back and he smelled like he'd overdone it with the Old Spice.

My mom chimed in. "Avery, honey, why not the new pink

cardigan I bought you? Why do you want to wear that silly old rag you love so much? 'Haste makes waste,' you know." She turned to my father. "I've bought her so many pretty sweaters, a whole rainbow of them hanging in her closet." This was another annoying habit they had. It was a constant competition between them, trying to demonstrate who was the better parent. In the mean time, they both fell short.

"Let's go, Avery. You ready?" Dad put out his hand for me. I hesitated, and then placed my hand in his. I was extra aware of my hand in his and kept wondering when I could let go.

He took me to my favorite restaurant. As we walked inside the glass doors into the dark interior, I heard the chatter of people and the clank of dishes and silverware. My mouth began to water as I eyed the well-lit dessert display at the front counter. There was a round cake with chocolate icing like the smooth surface of a freshly groomed skating rink. Next to that, there was a large fruit tart with a glossy coating and a thick carrot cake with billowy white icing. My dad steered me toward a table he thought would be best. I shoved my hands in my pockets so I would not rub them together.

I ordered the veggie enchiladas slathered with freshly chopped salsa. Dad ordered the chicken fried steak, the meal I remember he always ordered when I was a little girl.

"Honey, things like this happen all the time," he had said. I remember right after the divorce he had taken me here. I distinctly recall him saying between mouthfuls of battered steak and gravy, "Unfortunately, it's just a situation we'll have to make work. You know, problem-solve."

He had spoken to me like I was a member of his staff, not a nine-year old girl. I remember a lump in my throat, and being on the verge of tears.

Dad and I made awkward small talk while we waited for our meals. The waitress shimmied over to my dad's side of the table and kept smiling and leaning in too closely. Dad always drew the ladies. He beamed back when she set his platter of chicken fried steak before him.

She turned and said like I was an afterthought, a mere annoyance, "And there you go, you had the veggie enchiladas, right?"

I gave her a fake smile. She only had two orders to remember, was it really that hard? She reached across and placed my plate before me without out moving from her perch near my dad.

"And can I get you anything else at all?" she asked Dad with way too much enthusiasm.

"No, no. That will be all for now. Thank you. This looks magnificent." Dad kissed his fingers and pulled them away from his face in a magnanimous gesture. The waitress smiled, her eyes twinkled and she was off to the next table.

"So, Avery, I must know why you've been avoiding me for so long. I mean, what did I ever do? I called and called. You never called back." Dad cut a piece of steak and with his fork facing downward, dipped it in gravy, and ate it. This was a habit that used to drive my mom crazy. Dad had always waved her off saying that's how they ate in Europe. "I'd stop by and it would be the same way. What's the deal, Ave?" He asked with his cheeks full like a gerbil.

"The deal, Dad, is that you can't just pop into my life whenever it's convenient for you. That's all. Sorry, but that's how I feel." I stared him down, wishing this conversation would dissolve so I could enjoy the fresh cilantro salsa and enchiladas.

Dad was gesturing with the knife and fork, propped on the table ready to dive into the next bite. "What the heck do you mean Avery? Huh? I've always made an effort to be around. I love you more than anything, sweetie. You know that."

"I don't know that, Dad." I took a swig of my Diet Coke. "I know you left Mom and me high and dry for a new little family.

It's like you exchanged us for a younger, newer model. Don't you get it?"

Dad dropped his knife and fork and they clanked against his plate. A few drops of gravy spilled onto the white tablecloth. His face was turning red and his lips were pursed. "Now, who told you that? Your mother?"

"No, it's obvious, Dad. You left us for them. It's simple mathematics. It doesn't take a brain surgeon to figure that one out, Dad."

"Is that really what you think?" My dad folded his arms. "I've avoided telling you this all these years to protect you, Avery. I knew the relationship between you and your mom had to work, so..."

Breathe, just breathe, I told myself. I suddenly lost my appetite and felt a cold chill down my spine.

"I'm going to get in big trouble for telling you this, but I don't care anymore. It's high time you knew." In his eyes I couldn't tell if I saw kindness or measured coolness.

"Dad, you're scaring me. What is it?" My skin felt all prickly. My heart was pounding. People around me were having even conversations while my life was stuck in slow motion, a swirl of confusion. I focused on the white daisy in a crystal vase in the center of the table. I was trying to pinpoint something real.

"Your mom is the one who left me, Avery. Not the other way around."

My jaw dropped open. "What? What do you mean, Dad?" He wasn't saying this. He didn't mean what he was saying. This was another round in Mom and Dad's game of cat and mouse, with me stuck in the middle.

"It's true, Avery. I'm sorry. We both decided it was best if you didn't know since I couldn't take you to live with me at the time. I had a new marriage to think about. But honey, your mom is the one who called it quits first."

"I don't understand," I stammered. "How could that be? That's just crazy, Dad. You're being so weird." I felt like I was going to start sobbing uncontrollably and I didn't want to make a scene right there in the middle of the café.

"Your mom told me it was over six months before I left with Janet. I refused to leave. I thought we could work things out. She made me sleep on the couch all that time." Dad's face looked morose, like this had happened only yesterday. I felt a pit in my stomach as I remembered the rumpled blankets each morning on the monster couch as I headed out the door to catch the bus. I never thought anything of it.

"Yes, sweetie. I'm sorry, so sorry. You see, I'm not very good alone. I guess I just couldn't leave for good until I knew I had somebody else. I know how it looked, and I was okay with that. I didn't want you to hate your mom. If I took the blame that was all right if it eased the transition for you. I would've done anything to hold our family together."

My dad was talking but I was starting to have the strange sensation that I was floating out of my body. His voice sounded distant and I could no longer make out what he was saying. Nothing made sense anymore and even the daisy looked oddly out of place. How could you think your life is one way, and it turns out it's completely different?

I pushed back from the table, stunned, and stood up abruptly.

"I want to go. Now, Dad. Let's go."

"Now Avery, please honey, sit down and let's talk about this. I'm sure this is quite a blow to you." He had his hands in the air as if he might be able to put everything back together again if he just tried hard enough.

"No Dad. I'm leaving!" I shouted. I could feel the weight of the many stares in the restaurant. "I hate you both! You're crazy!"

I turned and ran out past a whirlwind of cakes and pastries

and out the glass doors. I ran down the steps and collapsed onto dad's car in the parking lot. Then I stood up and paced, sobbing, until I saw him slowly, defeated, walking across the parking lot to find me.

I leaned my head back and saw the very first snowflakes of the season floating down in drippy little drops from their great height. Funny how we never stop to think about how far a snowflake has to travel before it reaches us until we look up. Then it's a whole little world of diving, falling and crashing to the gravitational pull of the Earth.

Dear Lucrezia,

Maybe my whole life is one big lie. What else don't I know? All this time I've hated my father and blamed him for their break-up. My mother has played on everyone's sympathy, including mine, with the 'abandoned family' act. And that's all it was: an act. Why would she leave him? Why wouldn't she try to work it out? How did they keep it a secret from me for such a long time?

I'm starting to feel much older than my age with the weight of my life right now. Katelyn has asked me to be her birthing coach in the delivery room. How could I say no? I'm so afraid I'll fail her, that I'll steer her in the wrong direction. In one pivotal moment, she will have to decide the fate of her own and her baby's life. I know she wants to do the right thing. She's considering open adoption, but still says she can't make any promises.

I should be studying for my English Lit final right now but I can't concentrate. I wish I could stand on top of the Duomo in Florence with a birds-eye view of the world where the little figurines below walk in fairly predictable directions and their lives seem to make perfect sense.

Avery

8

The snow that had formed a thick blanket of solitude around our house on I Street two weeks ago was now an ashen crust. I wished another storm would come along, like new white paint on a dingy room, and brighten my surroundings. I reveled in the massive snowplows that would come seemingly out of nowhere and swoosh by in a low, steady hum. I enjoyed the laborious job of clearing the sidewalks in slow, steady scrapes. The piles of heavy snow were pillows that softened the harsh sounds of the world. It was an excuse to sleep and be still. Heavy snowstorms gave me the urge to hibernate and lose myself in mugs full of cinnamon hot chocolate.

But this morning, the white, winter blanket outside was gone. Winter's ugly stepsister, the inversion, hovered overhead. The air was biting cold. The dirty snow that lingered in the frigid temperatures felt like a suffocating trap from which I couldn't escape. My mom had been knocking on my bedroom door on and off for several hours.

"Sweetie," she had said. "Please open up. We need to talk. Let's work this out. I can explain everything." Then she knocked with greater force: POUND, POUND, POUND. "Avery. Open your door this instant. You can't shut me out forever."

I wished that I could've shut her out forever. I loved my mother. Don't get me wrong. But how could I've been such a fool for so many years? All this time I had excused my mother's worst behavior because Dad left her. I felt sorry for her. It was all just a farce. My dad took the blame. I figured if he had been around to help and make her happy she wouldn't have been so ornery and difficult to live with. We wouldn't have had to wait four weeks for the telephone company to turn our phone back on when my mom couldn't pay the bills. When I was sad, I would've had Daddy there to rub my feet with lotion, like he did when I was little, and tell me I was his 'gorgeous little girl.' Most of all, I reasoned, we would've still been a family. I had created a wall of hatred for my dad that was so tall, wide and opaque that I could not see through it to the truth, until now.

I hugged my knees to my chest and gently rocked back and forth on the floor of my bedroom. Tigger's slender body and thick, winter fur warmed my side. Outside my window, it was gray and gloomy. The inversion had turned the atmosphere over like a pancake holding in fog and pollution and keeping out the sunlight like a widow's veil. A few crystalline flakes drifted down from the heavens. But it wasn't enough to clear up the smog. We needed another good storm. It was Sunday, which added to the silence outside my frozen window. There would be no children playing in the hardened snow, no busy parents headed off to work or to complete errands. The Sabbath, along with the heavy snowstorm, made our neighborhood seem frozen in the stillness of the moment. Soon I would see families buttoning their little ones' thick coats and skirting them off to church down the street.

I combed my hair with my fingers. It had become long and oddly thicker in the process of growing it out, no stringiness like I'd expected. I hadn't cut it since last summer. Red, wispy curls were spilling onto my back.

My stomach growled. I was becoming ravenous. Sooner or later I would have to come out of my room.

"Avery?" My mom's voice was tentative this time through

my thin bedroom door. "It's time to get ready for church, dear. Avery?" She softly knocked and then I could tell she was leaning up against my door. How could she be so casual, so normal, after everything? I felt betrayed by my own mother. "I made your favorite," she continued. "Hot chocolate with marshmallows and just a touch of cinnamon."

Tigger perked up her raggedy ear and pointed her snout in the direction of the smell of rich cocoa and spice.

"I'm not going! Leave me alone!" I yelled.

I waited for my mom to snap back, to fire back an insult through the wooden barrier that separated us. But she remained cool.

"All right. I'll leave it on the tray outside your door." She tapped the door gently. "I wish you'd come out of there and get ready for church," she called. "I wish you'd talk to me."

My Mom was no fun to fight with when she was acting all reasonable. I wondered if she was up to something, or if this was a sign that she was genuinely sorry for deceiving me all those years. The silence outside my door told me that it was safe enough to retrieve my hot chocolate. Just as promised, she had left a little tray on the carpet. Steam rose from my favorite mug amidst smooth, swirling marshmallows sprinkled with the sweet, woodsy aroma of cinnamon. I was eight years old again and the world was safe and full of possibilities. It was safe to dream. Funny how familiar scents can bring about such strong emotions.

When I was finished, I opened my door and left the tray outside, like you do at hotels, turning back to the security of my room. Before I could shut the door behind me, I felt the force of it being pushed open behind me. I swung around and saw my mom's exasperated gaze. She had dyed her hair a honey blond sometime in the last few days. I had to admit that it was her most flattering shade yet. The golden highlights around her face softened her. I still noticed some dark circles underneath her eyes though, and crows' feet at the edges of her expertly lined eyes. She looked tired.

I felt the impulse to push her out of my room, away from me, far out of my space, out of my life.

Mom said, "May I come in, please?" Her exhausted eyes were pleading with me. Again, her rationality took me by surprise.

I turned toward my bed and sat down. Tigger jumped up to my side like she was ready to defend me.

We were quiet a long time. Mom stared out the window and traced my name with her pointer finger in the moisture that had gathered on the windowpane because of the cold. Then, she took a deep breath and turned to face me.

"I'm sorry, Avery. It was a long time ago and your dad and I thought it was best if you didn't know the whole story at the time."

I felt the weight of her as she sat on the edge of my bed.

"How could you, Mom? How could you lie to your only daughter all these years?"

"Honey, we didn't mean to lie. You just assumed Daddy left us and, well, I didn't correct that assumption. That's all. I knew you wouldn't understand. You were such a daddy's girl already. And he couldn't take you, honey, as much as he wanted to. He worked such long hours. We thought it was best if you were on my side." She looked down at her feet. "It was actually a very selfless act on his part, him letting you believe that he was to blame."

"But all these years, I've been so angry at Dad! And at Janet. I should've been angry at you!" I shrieked.

"Avery," her voice remained calm. "Adult relationships are complicated. Looking back," my mom stared into the distance at another time, "I wish your dad and I could've worked it out. I wish that I had tried harder. I messed up. At the time, it was so impossible to ever picture us happy together again." She touched the window and underlined my name with her finger. "Just like now when it's covered in snow outside, and so dreary, it's hard to ever picture it sunny and hot out there again."

"But why, Mom?" I was wounded. "Why did you tell him to go? How could you turn away from him like that, from us? What did he ever do?"

She touched my forehead with her fingertips. They were cold as ice and I recoiled.

"It's so hard to explain, Avie. We just fell apart. It had been years since I felt like he really listened to me. We simply went through the motions of life, pretending. I couldn't do that anymore. I had had enough." She stared off to that faraway place again. "He worked longer hours at the office," she continued. "Some weeks I never even saw him. He would come home too exhausted to even talk to me. I tried. For a long time I tried. I was so lonely after being home all day taking care of you. I just wanted to connect, you know, talk to my husband. But he wouldn't, he couldn't give me anything anymore, he had nothing left. In a way, he left long before I asked him to."

"Does that make you feel better, Mom? Huh? To always blame him like you do? Even now? Isn't it time to at least be honest? I don't know what, or who, to believe anymore." I buried my head in my pillow to hide my tears.

"Avie, I'm sorry," she touched my back. "Like I said, dear, it was such a long time ago." She stroked my hair. "Sometimes I wish I could go back and try harder. I certainly would have, if I had known how hard it was going to be. I didn't, though, Avie. I can't go back. Gosh, wouldn't it be great if we could go back and erase our mistakes in life? Just presto—like that?" She lifted my face up from the soggy pillow and held it in her hands. "I do know this, Avery. I have always loved you with all my heart. I know I've failed you in so many ways. But the love has always been there, always will be. How can I ever make things right with you, Avie?"

Her question hung in the air like a thick fog. I shrugged my shoulders and lay back on my bed studying the ceiling.

"Can't we just put it all behind us now? Move on?" she asked.

She sounded like she was a million miles away.

Then my mom did something so uncharacteristic of her that it frightened me a little. She lay down next to me on the bed, right next to me, with our arms touching. I had never noticed how similar in size we were. Our feet stretched out to nearly the same length and our body shapes looked similar. I had always thought of my mother as so distant, so much taller and thinner, so unlike me.

Her voice was cool and calm. "You know, they don't give you a manual at the hospital when they hand you the baby. Kids don't come with instructions, unfortunately." Mom blew air through her lips that puffed her blond bangs into the air. "We're all just doing it blindly. Trying to do the best we can with what we know."

I couldn't move a muscle. I was uncomfortable with her close. Even Tigger appeared to be perplexed. So I remained there, like a statue, waiting for her next move.

"Tell me this, Avery. Why are you always so angry with me?"

"I'm not always angry with you, Mom." I weighed each word carefully like I was walking on a fragile sheet of ice on a frozen pond. Slow and steady, don't make any sudden movements, I told myself.

"Every time I try to help you, you take it so personally and get so upset. I don't understand it."

"Take it personally?" I was exasperated. "Well, I should think so. You're my mother. Anything you say to me goes straight to my heart. How could I take it any way but personally, Mom?"

I sat up too quickly and felt dizzy from all the blood rushing to my head.

Mom sat up too, mirroring my movements. "I just want to

help you avoid problems in life. I figure if I can warn you, tell you things to help you improve yourself, your life will be easier in the long run."

"It doesn't help, Mom. It just makes me feel about two inches tall." I twirled my hair around my finger. "If anything, it makes me not want to try at all, to just, I don't know, disappear. I feel like I'm never good enough, never worthy enough."

"What? Never worthy enough? Of course you are! Is that truly what you think? That you're not good enough?"

"Well, yeah, Mom. You're always criticizing my hair, my weight, my choices. Even the people who I hang out with."

"'Stupid is as stupid does' though, Avie."

"See? See what I mean? What's with your clichés? I hate your clichés. Loathe them." I crinkled up my face.

Mom was undeterred. "My mom, Grams, has always been tough on me. But through it all I know she's just showing her love. It's all that I know how to do."

"But did you like it, Mom? Do you remember how she made you feel, how she still makes you feel?"

"Well, no. Of course I didn't—don't like it. It hurts. But maybe it has made me better, strong enough to withstand the hardships of raising you alone. I think I'm tougher because of it. Everything she says has a partial truth to it. Of course, I guess that's why it's so painful."

"Shouldn't the ones who love you the most build you up?" I asked. "You know, 'accentuate the positive?' Maybe the greatest gift you can give your child is a healthy self-esteem. Not that I'm any sort of parenting expert or anything."

"Oh no. But you'll get there one day, then, one day you'll understand." There was disdain on her tongue.

"Will I, Mom? Because I can't imagine saying to my child some of the things you've said to me. I really can't. Sometimes your words really crush my spirit."

"I know you'll earn all those compliments that you long for, one day, Avery, from your employers, your husband, your friends and colleagues. You'll appreciate them so much more and you won't have a big head."

I turned and looked at her straight in her overly made-up blue eyes. I accentuated every single word. "Mom, I need to hear the good things from you most of all. What you say matters more than anybody."

My mom was quiet. She took a deep breath, turned toward the door, and then back to me. She stepped a little closer and fidgeted. She looked uncomfortable and nervous.

"Listen to me, Avery Rose. You are a brilliant girl, with a joyous, resilient spirit. And Avery, you are becoming, well, a beautiful young woman. Don't you ever forget it."

I felt something like butterflies in my stomach and tingles all over. I wanted to run down I Street and shout to the world what my mom had said to me. I wanted to run down the side streets and out of the Avenues onto South Temple. I would stand in the street, put my hand up to the cars with a large gesture like The Supremes and say, "Stop! My Mom thinks I'm great! She really thinks I'm great!" Then I'd run and shout loud enough for the whole world to hear, until the sound of my voice reached all the way up to Heaven.

❧❦❧❦

It felt soothing to go to church. Sometimes it's just the solace you need, the best therapy. I felt a new peace and calm as I sat on the wooden pew. The talks the speakers gave touched my soul. It made me wonder how much the eloquence of the talk has to do with the listener, rather than the speaker. So many times, I sat in our chapel and felt nothing but boredom. This particular Sunday I felt like God may very well have been in the room with us. As

I sang the hymns, I could feel a warm feeling in my chest and emotion rising through me. I wanted to cry, but this time, for joy instead of sadness. For the overwhelming sense of love and contentment I felt. I belonged.

Mom and I still had a long way to go before winning any sort of mother or daughter of the year award. I was certain it wouldn't be long before the old habits came out, rearing their ugly heads. A painful insult would no doubt shoot out of her mouth headed straight for me, as usual. I know giving me those honest compliments was extremely difficult for her. Still, my saying to her face how I felt was freeing. And she seemed to get it. She seemed to truly care. Maybe she had always cared. Life has a way of making our habits grow stronger over time, the good ones and the bad ones. Over time, I wanted to become nicer and more understanding of others, not the other way around. If I could wish it and try hard enough, maybe it would be so.

Grams was in pink mode at Sacrament Meeting, and I don't mean pale pink like a summer rose, more like pink Pepto-Bismol. She wore a hot pink hat with a feather in it that was oddly aligned with her sharp chin, a flamingo pink blouse, a cotton-candy skirt, a ruby pink belt, and her rose petal pumps that matched her long, dangly earrings. Grams sat in between Papa and my mom. As she looked around the congregation, there was judgment in Grams' eyes. She always had the skinny on ward gossip.

I sat next to Mom. She had her honey blond hair pulled back in a neat ponytail and her makeup was light and natural. Mom looked pretty. There was a new tenderness emanating between us. And though I knew we had a lot more stuff to talk about, I believed we were onto a little miracle ourselves in our lonely little house on I Street.

Dear Lucrezia,
Tonight when I visited Katelyn, I saw something new

and deeply troubling in her eyes. She could deliver this baby any day and I think she's terrified. All the false confidence had disappeared. I tried to reassure her, saying that the doctors know what they're doing, that babies get born healthy every single day. Still, I think her fear extended beyond the physical birth into the decision.

I don't know what to tell her to do. It's such a complicated life choice. I am glad I'm not in her shoes, and yet, my heart aches for her. She was quiet as I sat there with her at her home tonight. In her eyes, I saw the same look Tigger gets when the vet lifts her up on the cold metal table in his office to give her shots. It's a look of primal, animal fear. It's dangerous. A scared person cannot think clearly. She hardly said two words to me the whole night.

You won't believe the conversation I had with my mom this morning before church. I was so brave. I know you'd be proud. I'd never really opened up and faced her like that, with real honesty before and told her exactly how I felt. But I feel so relieved now, like we were onto something new and wondrous.

I'm picking Barclay up at the airport tomorrow morning. He's coming home for winter break. I can't wait to see him. He hasn't written to me in weeks, just phoned a few days ago to ask if I could pick him up. I don't know why he's acting so strange. Sometimes I wonder if the same tendency that led his mother to do what she did, the awful darkness, resides somewhere in Barclay, too. Is he capable of doing what she did?

I've missed him so. The first thing I will do when I see him is reach up and rustle his long, thick mop of hair. And then I will hug him tightly and not want to let go.

Love,

Avery

9

Katelyn peered out her bedroom window with gloomy eyes. The wall-length mirror behind her that was framed by old cheerleading photos and snapshots with friends were artifacts from a different lifetime. With her pinkie finger, Katelyn scooped some lip-gloss out of a small round tub and applied it to her lips. Then she quickly checked out the window again. It was a sorry sight. She should've been looking out that window waiting for a date to pick her up and take her to the movies, instead of biding her time before the potential parents of her unborn baby arrived. She rubbed her belly lovingly. "They should be here any minute. How do I look?" She asked.

"Beautiful," I answered. Her cheeks had some nice, peachy-pink color in them today. She'd curled her hair with a curling iron and applied some concealer underneath her eyes.

"Oh yeah, real beautiful," she said, motioning down at her pregnant girth.

"I mean it. You do, Katelyn."

We heard a car pull up and I ran to the window beside her. A big guy wearing a freshly pressed white linen shirt, lavender tie, and wrinkled pants got out of the back seat of the sedan. Faint stubble outlined his strong jaw. He smiled lovingly and opened the passenger door. Out stepped a stunning tan woman with curly, blond hair tied back in a low ponytail with a large cornflower blue hairtie. Her dress was a slightly lighter hue. She took his hand and smiled a large, hopeful grin. The two followed the social worker up the sidewalk toward the front door, a portly woman in a well-worn gray blazer and skirt with a white silk blouse and sensible shoes. She walked with conviction, and had deep worry lines on her forehead and around her mouth.

Katelyn insisted her parents not be here for this meeting. After a lot of convincing, they finally acquiesced.

The doorbell rang. Katelyn closed her eyes and looked heavenward. Then she opened the door.

"You're not late," she told them, glancing at her watch.

"Well, this is pretty important. I guess miracles really do still happen," Mallory smiled so big we could see her pink gums. "Even I could be on time."

"Thankfully," Buddy said, grinning with relief, revealing his pronounced overbite. "But I forgot to iron my pants last night, sorry, and Mal needed some help this morning. So, here we are." He looked down at his wrinkled pants and shifted nervously. His forehead was shiny with sweat. "We're just so happy to be here. Thanks for asking to meet us."

I smiled warmly and extended my hand. "You must be Buddy and Mallory. I'm Avery Rose, Katelyn's friend. Nice to meet you both."

"Nice to meet you," the Carters chimed in unison, nodding their heads politely.

"And this is Katelyn," I offered.

"Hello, Katelyn," Mallory said, her eyes shining and her voice syrupy smooth.

Buddy extended his hand toward Katelyn. "It's so nice to meet you. I can't tell you how much it would mean to us—if you chose us," his voice quivered. "We'd be so happy."

The Carters studied Katelyn with looks of wonder.

The social worker intervened, "I'm Ms. Lundhausen," she said coolly. "Shall we get this interview started?"

Katelyn welcomed them into the immaculate living room. Her mother spent the day before cleaning in preparation for the visit. If her daughter wouldn't let her be here for the meeting, she had said, she'd still find a way to contribute, however small it might be.

Katelyn whispered into my ear, "Let Tigger in." I looked at her quizzically, unsure why she'd want exuberant Tigg drooling all over her houseguests. Buddy and Mallory remained smiling but appeared to be unsure of what we were talking about and more nervous than before.

"Can I get you something to drink?" I offered.

"A glass of water would be great, thank you," said Buddy, wiping his brow.

"I don't think we have any candy bars, sorry." Katelyn teased.

Both Buddy and Mallory laughed a little too heartily. Mrs. Lundhausen remained expressionless.

"You've done your homework," Buddy smiled. "No worries. I'm trying to cut back anyway," he said, patting his small pooch.

I opened the back door and Tigger bounded in, jumping up on Buddy's lap and licking Mallory's face. Mrs. Lundhausen sprung up from her seat with alarm.

"Oh, hi, there. Thanks for the kisses." Mallory cooed while Tigger licked her cheeks.

Buddy scratched Tigger's bent ear. "What a beautiful dog!"

Katelyn beamed.

After Tigger settled down at Buddy and Mal's feet, Katelyn got down to business.

"Why do you want a baby?" She asked pointedly.

Mal took a deep breath, glanced at Buddy, who nodded his head with reassurance. Then she spoke. "We have so much love to give. All my life I've wanted to be a mother. It's all I've ever wanted to be. I have my prince charming, my lovely home, I want to share all this bounty with a baby." A fat tear rolled down her cheek. "I have an ache in my soul for a baby to love."

"And we would love your baby with every fiber of our beings," Buddy sniffed back tears. "We're not perfect. I'm the first to admit that. But we love each other more than words can say. We love life, too, and all the beauty in it. There's always beauty. No matter how difficult circumstances can be, if you look for joy, you'll find it. We always look for the joy. And we try hard, we show up for things, we attend church every Sunday, and we never give up. We'd never let her down."

"Did you say her?" Katelyn asked, her eyes large like two saucers.

"Or him," Buddy corrected himself. "Of course we'd be happy with either a boy or a girl." Then, he looked at his wife with measured caution and continued. "It's just that Mal has had this funny feeling that we'll be adopting a girl."

❧❧

It was morning and I was going to be late to the airport if I didn't leave right then. I dug through my closet to find my favorite sweater, the old chunky one that my mom hated. I couldn't find it anywhere. A cotton candy pink cardigan lay at the bottom of dirty clothes I had searched through in desperation. Mom had bought it for me last summer and I had thrown it immediately on the floor of my closet. She knew I liked muted tones for clothing, but still, she persisted. Why was I so nervous about picking up Barclay? Barc was my oldest friend in the world and here I was fretting around in a nervous rush. He certainly never cared what I wore. I reached for my black turtleneck, charcoal tailored pants, and then I pulled on the pink sweater, cursing my mother, and leaving it unbuttoned. Then I dabbled some rouge on my cheeks and ran a brush through my long hair. The clock was ticking.

Tigger eyed me with curiosity.

The neighborhood was motionless and eerily still. I reached for my thick winter coat and pulled it on as I walked toward my car in the driveway and fumbled around in the pockets for my keys. I couldn't find them so I ran back inside and felt on top of the endless piles of magazines and mail in the kitchen for them, to no avail. I headed into the dark living room in a frenzy, overturning the huge cushions of the monster couch. I was going to be late.

"Mom." I called. "Have you seen my keys? I can't find them anywhere."

My mom appeared in the hallway wearing a cream-colored terrycloth robe and a matching towel wrapped around her head. Her face shone with a new coat of lotion.

"Where are you going so early?"

"I told you," I said, tossing pillows, pulling up cushions. "I have to go pick up Barclay from the airport. If I could just find my stupid keys."

"Oh. Him." Mom pulled the robe tightly closed around her in a gesture that emanated disapproval.

I stopped, exasperated, and looked up at her. "Mom, please don't start. Okay? I thought we made some, you know, major progress the other day. Please don't ditch my best friend."

"What? What did I do this time?" She was digging through the stacks of books and knick-knacks on the cluttered shelves at the edge of the living room, an expert packrat going through her treasures.

She asked, "When did you have them last?"

"Well, if I knew that, I wouldn't be in this predicament, now would I, Mom?" I knew I shouldn't be talking to her this way, with such disrespect, but old habits die-hard. Plus, I never have been good under pressure.

"Ah-ha!" Mom grinned, though it was hard to tell since her

lips had nearly disappeared without any lipstick to define them. "Just call me: 'Mom, the finder of lost things.' You complain about me hanging on to stuff, but you must admit, I have a gift when it comes to finding things in all of it."

"Thanks, Mom. Where were they?" I asked with a sigh.

"Under the coffee table." Mom handed them to me. "I've got to get ready for work. Don't want to be late and make Mr. Blackwell angry. What are you and Barclay going to do?"

"I dunno, Mom. Can we talk about this later? I'm late."

I didn't wait for her reply. I ran to the car, pulled out of our driveway, angry with myself for not bringing gloves. The steering wheel was a ring of ice on my fingers. I pulled the sleeves of my coat over my wrists to try and create a buffer against the cold. The defrost system in my ancient junky car took an eternity to warm up. Today I simply didn't have time to wait. So I hunched down in my seat as I drove down I Street so I could see through the clear space at the bottom of the icy windshield. These were not safe driving conditions, especially with the slick streets, and I knew it. But I didn't care. I was headed to see Barclay.

The airport was quiet and sparsely dotted with travelers at this early hour. I saw a tall figure underneath the Delta Airlines sign in a long brown coat dancing a little jig to stay warm. He stopped when he saw me in my clunky, unmistakable car. Barclay's hair was longer and curlier than when I had seen him off to MIT last fall. His thick mop of hair hung low over his eyes until the sub-zero wind whipped it up and away from his face. As I pulled up beside him and waved through the window, I saw in his hazel eyes, staring back at me, something that looked a lot like joy.

Barclay's physique had filled out in the months he had been away in Massachusetts. He looked much stronger. I threw my car into park and jumped out of the driver's seat. I ran up to him and wrapped my arms around his layers: two awkward Eskimos trying to embrace. As I hugged him close to me, I could feel the warmth of his cheek on mine. He felt sturdy and comfortable. Barclay was home!

"Let me look at you," he said. I felt myself blush. I still couldn't figure out where the butterflies in my stomach were coming from. He pushed away and stared at my face. I tried to smooth my long hair down in the wind.

"You look beautiful, Avery. Just beautiful. Your hair is longer. I like it." He hugged me again.

"Thanks, Barclay. You look great, too. You're bigger or something." I couldn't stop smiling. "Oh, Barc, I missed you so much!" I grabbed his gloved hand and he instantly grasped mine back.

He put his big duffle bag in my small trunk. Then he squeezed himself into the passenger seat. As we drove away from the airport, I noticed he was resting his left arm up behind me. His close proximity felt good and easy, like finding my favorite sweater after all. When I gazed back and forth from the road to his big, hazel eyes, I felt a little jittery and at a loss for words. We were quiet for a few minutes, which felt like hours. Finally, I spoke while keeping my eyes on the road ahead of me.

"So, how are you?" I asked.

"I'm good, Avery, really good. Even better now that you're here. I really missed you."

"I missed you, too," I said, trying to lighten the heaviness of his tone. What was happening here? "I was starting to worry," I continued. "I hadn't heard from you in weeks. Everything okay?"

"Yeah, yeah. I'm sorry. It's just, well, I thought it would be better if we both had some time to think, you know, sort things out? Especially you."

"I'm not sure what you mean," I said defensively. "So, you weren't just busy with school? Studying for finals? You meant to not call me back?" I felt like I had been socked in the gut.

"It's not like that, Avery. I just wanted to give you some space so you can see how you feel."

"What? Why? I know how I feel. You're my best friend in the whole world. You better not be deserting me, Barclay." I sounded desperate, not a tone I liked to hear in my own voice.

I pulled onto North Temple, headed for home. A thin layer of ice coated the streets. The thermostat froze to single-digit temperatures over night. We remained stuck in the depressing haze of the inversion. I made myself take it slow, though my mounting anger and hurt nearly drove me to push harder on the gas pedal.

"All this time, I just figured MIT was tough and you needed all your time for studying. You wrote me every week at first and then nothing," I said, with a wounded puppy dog voice.

"Avery, why don't we talk about this later? It's just so good to see you."

"No—Barclay. I want to talk about this now." I slapped the steering wheel with one of my hands. "If you don't want to hang out with me anymore, I need to know. I've had enough people in my life disappoint me. You, of all people, should know that. You won't believe what my Mom did, totally lied to me about my dad leaving us. Turns out, she's the one who ordered him out of the house, long before he left." I paused, took a deep breath, tried to get a hold of myself. "I'm forgiving her, though, I guess. I'm trying to. Mom and I have sort of made an 'amazing breakthrough.' Whatever. We'll see if it lasts. Anyway, it's a long story. I can't believe you're doing this to me."

Though I was slow and steady on the icy road, emotionally I was spinning out of control.

"Avie, Avie. It's all right. Please don't get upset. I didn't call because I wanted you to become sure about how you felt about me. That's all. I thought you needed some time and a clear head, without me bugging you all the time."

We were in the Avenues now and the neighborhood was

beginning to wake up. Several people were scraping their slippery walks and a few kids clad in hats, huge coats, mittens and boots headed for the bus stops.

I continued, "You're acting weird, Barclay. What's going on here?" I felt that same lonely, helpless feeling as when I was a little girl and my dad stood at the door with his suitcases neatly packed, looking back at me with tears streaming down his face. Suddenly, I wanted out of the car. "Wait a sec. Where am I supposed to be taking you? Your dad lives in Sandy now. Wow, I was just driving to your house on instinct. They painted it, you know, the new owners. With sage green trim. It's really pretty, actually. I guess they're totally remodeling the inside, too." I hoped my comment hurt him in some way.

"It had been needing it for years," he said, calmly. "Why don't we just go to your place? I'm not sure I'm ready to see my dad yet, anyway. Is that all right with you?"

My house nearly disappeared in the dirty snow that surrounded it. I drove up the steep incline of our driveway with speed. I knew I needed the momentum to get up the icy slope.

I parked the car and reached for the handle of the door. At the same time, he reached for my shoulder and stopped me.

"Wait. Wait just a minute. Okay, Avery? I wanted to do this later, but here we are, talking about you and me. No better time than the present, I suppose." Was Barclay sweating? How could he be hot? He took off his gloves and put his hands in mine. They felt soft and warm.

"Avery." He looked into my eyes with such seriousness. There was so much depth in his hazel eyes I had never noticed. "I have loved you my whole life. You mean everything to me."

"Awe, Barclay, I feel the same way."

"No, Avery. I mean—I'm in love with you. Always have been. Always will be. It's always been you. Only you."

He leaned over and before I had time to react his lips were on mine in two gentle kisses that made me tingle all the way from my lips to my toes. I couldn't believe what was happening. My timid friend had made such a bold move. His affection startled me, but it also felt right and soothing. Much to my surprise, I wanted him to kiss me again.

The whole day we puttered around the house. We were both extremely anxious. We knew we were treading new ground here. It was so strange kissing him like that.

I mean, this was the same guy who I played dominoes with on our back patio when I was eight years old. I remember when the tooth fairy came to his house for the very first time. Barclay had always been a vital part of my life and my rocky childhood. I never dreamed it could turn into something more.

The kiss felt perfect and, well, glorious.

I had practiced kissing myself in the mirror throughout my early teens, tipping my head just so while standing on tiptoe on our linoleum floor. I would pretend the image I saw in the mirror was Sean Baker, the cutest guy at my middle school. I tried to open my mouth a little like I saw them do on soap operas, though I had no idea why anyone would want to kiss that way. All I knew was that if Sean aimed his beautiful lips toward mine, I'd be ready.

Because I'd never been kissed in all those years, I'd built up sort of a phobia of kissing. I had no idea if I'd ever be any good at it or if I would even like doing it. The bathroom mirror can only give you so much practice. The two quick kisses with Barclay were gentle, petal soft, and heavenly.

***

Mom was busy moving her piles and making taller stacks on the kitchen counter, and on chairs in the dining room.

After the first cordial niceties, she pretended Barclay wasn't there and reached around him to grab a stack of dated mail and put it on top of another stash of magazines. Barclay didn't seem bothered by this at all. He was used to being invisible to people in his life.

Barclay asked me if I wanted to go to a movie with him that evening. The invitation sounded wonderful to me. To escape into a dark movie theater with a large tub of salty, buttered popcorn with him next to me, so safe and warm, was an inviting prospect, to say the least. But my dad was coming to get me. I told Barclay I couldn't go. He was disappointed, but also understanding and supportive. We rescheduled for another night, and I drove him to his dad's house. He kissed me softly on the lips, both of us lingering face to face long after the kiss was finished.

Barclay had always been so supportive. He knew that I needed to see my dad. I guess once I knew that my father wasn't to blame for all of our problems, it should've set our relationship on a new course. But my dad and I had been doing this dance for so many years now that it had become habitual. I didn't know how to relate to him without being adversarial.

There were times I wished I could just rise out of my body and make myself behave the way I knew I should. I guess this is what the whole maturity thing is all about. Maybe growing up means practicing self-control and making life what you want it to be, while accepting people for who they are.

Sometimes I felt ancient at eighteen. I swore that occasionally there was an ache in my heart that extended to my back and made me hunch over and walk around stiffly like a little old lady.

When I saw my dad standing there at the front door, the way he looked took me aback. He was disheveled. His blue dress shirt was wrinkled underneath his black wool coat. Dad was unshaven with a dark shadow around his strong jaw and his hair was sticking up in soft, unruly wisps. Dad looked like he had dropped everything to make sure he was on time to see me.

Before my dad had arrived that night, I was confused and felt a pounding headache looming, and a fogginess surrounding my thoughts about Barclay. That pang of missing him returned, even though I knew I'd see him again soon. And then I worried about how the conversation would go with my dad. Something like, "Oh, hi, Dad, how are ya? Sorry I've blamed all my problems on you for the past ten years. Anyhow, pretty snow out there, isn't it?" Does Hallmark make a card for that?

I was ashamed about hating him for so long that I couldn't help but grieve for the lost, wasted time when I really needed him but pushed him away. Perhaps Dad would've tried harder to have been a part of my life if I hadn't been so hard on him, so hateful. After all, I had misplaced the blame, putting it squarely on his shoulders. That was a large load to haul. I still could hardly believe that my mom had forced him out of our lives all those years ago.

After so much worry, when I saw him, I ran toward him and put my arms around him. He smelled faintly of Old Spice and mint toothpaste mixed with the musty scent of leaves. Dad felt so strong. His burdened shoulders were still wide and sturdy. I felt like someone was pouring a cool, soothing salve over our aching wounds. We swayed together there, holding each other.

Then we walked arm in arm through the crusty, frozen snow. With each step our shoes cracked open the slick, frozen top layer, crumbling into the softer snow still barely intact underneath. Though my nose and lips were frozen and our breath visible as we walked in the cold night, I felt warm and content. My dad put one of his big, sturdy hands on my shoulder and led me back toward the car. The stars were bright in the black, winter sky, seemingly smiling down upon us.

Dear Lucrezia,

You won't believe this, but Barclay kissed me twice. It was strange and exhilarating all at the same time. The second time left me wanting more. He also told me he loves me, that he's always loved me. I know that I love Barclay, too. But how do I know what kind of love it is? If I don't return Barclay's romantic feelings, will I lose my best friend forever?

I was upset and worried about what to say the next time I saw my dad. I blamed him for everything for so long. Turns out, I didn't need to say anything at all

Katelyn's meeting with the Carters could not have gone better. She told me later that she asked me to let Tigger in because she wanted to see how they treated her. "You can tell a lot about someone by how they treat animals," she said. Katelyn adored Mal and Buddy. They stayed for two hours. Katelyn felt a strong connection to them. She told me they would be ideal parents for her baby, if only she could give her up.

As much as she loved them, she's growing increasingly desperate to keep her baby. I think she is blinded by her love for the child growing in her womb. She's convinced that her love will be enough

I can't believe I'm going to be her coach in the delivery room. I'm not ready to see something like that. I've already told her 'yes' and I can't turn my back on her now. I'm praying for strength.

Love,
Avery

10

Our relationship had changed and we could never go back to just being friends. I got a sinking feeling when I went and picked up the phone to return Barclay's calls. Usually, I'd just hang the receiver back up. I don't know if it was just normal jitters that were gripping me inside, or a red flag waving telling me this romantic relationship with him just wasn't right for me. I knew I didn't want to hurt my dear friend. Not that what happened between us was a mistake. It's just that friendship was so much easier to navigate than these new, deep feelings that were emerging inside of me.

The crevasse between Katelyn and her parents grew wider each day. They were encouraging her to pursue an open adoption with the Carters. "You love them," her mother told her. "You said yourself that they feel like family already. They would be excellent parents for your baby. You could still be involved in your baby's life and go to college, meet a good church member, and get married in the temple. Those dreams could be alive!" But Katelyn was silent and slammed her bedroom door on her mom, who spoke to her in muffled tones through the door. "We want what's best for you and for your baby, that's all. This is painful for us, too."

Katelyn couldn't see why they expected her to give her baby up for adoption. Mrs. Lundhausen from LDS social services called and talked to Katelyn every other day. She was feeling the intense pressure and it showed. The circles under her eyes were coming back, growing darker each day. While her belly blossomed, the rest of her seemed to be shrinking and shriveling under the stress. Katelyn told me that she couldn't possibly return home after her baby was born if she kept her. But where would she go?

The vaulted ceiling in my dad's living room was filled to the brim with a majestic, 18-foot-tall blue spruce bedecked with wide, cranberry satin ribbons, white lights and berry garland. A glittering gold angel sat on the tip-top of the magnificent tree.

It was Christmas Eve. I finally agreed to spend the holidays with him, Janet, and my half siblings Casey and Cole. I guess I owed my dad that much, having misjudged him for so many years. The trip to Italy seemed like eons ago. Grams and Papa had talked Mom into going to St. George with them, which was just fine with me.

Casey and Cole ripped open their presents with unabashed glee. Casey got a new Barbie and accompanying horse, and Cole got a set of Power Rangers action figures.

I tried to act excited when Dad handed me a slick, rectangular present wrapped in hunter green paper and tied in a silver bow. We had never done it this way before, opened presents on Christmas Eve. It must've been Janet's idea. I tried to pretend this unfamiliar tradition was not strange to me, but it was.

I wished I felt something for Casey and Cole as I watched them smashing up all the satiny wrapping paper on the ground into large wads, throwing it into the air like autumn leaves. They were adorable little kids. But they seemed more like cute neighbor kids, not a half brother and sister. This was going to take time.

"Go ahead—open it," Dad said. His face was full of expectation. I wanted to please him, to make up for lost time. "Go on, don't be shy. This is your home, too."

Dad was beaming. He looked so content with all three of his children finally under one roof for the holidays. His hair was slicked back. He wore a red argyle sweater with brown corduroy pants and polished leather shoes. I'm not sure I'd ever seen Dad that happy before.

He leaned forward in his easy chair as I delicately opened the paper at its seams. Even Casey and Cole were quiet while I opened the box and dug through the mounds of crumply tissue paper. Guilt settled in my stomach as I looked at them. Here they were almost six and seven and I didn't even know their favorite colors or what they hoped to find in their Christmas stockings in the morning.

A fire was crackling in the stone fireplace, emitting a soothing scent that smelled like hickory. Every now and then the fire would pop as snow from the storm outside drifted through the chimney. Then the hot yellow flame hungrily licked the iron of the fireplace, roaring with new life.

"I love it." I said, without conviction. I held up a pale pink cashmere beret and matching cardigan sweater. I pictured myself looking hideous in it.

"You know," said Dad, grinning expectantly, "Like they wear in *Italia*." He tried his best at an Italian accent, but failed miserably. Right then, I missed the painter with the caramel skin and deep wrinkles who had befriended me.

I put on the downy soft beret and tipped it to the left as I supposed Italians used to do in the old days. I draped the sweater over my shoulders and struck a pose. "What do you think? How very vogue, right?"

"Wow," Casey said, stroking my shoulder. "You look really pretty." Cole ran circles around us, squealing with delight. I grabbed a hold of him, and then caught Casey with my other arm, and tumbled to the ground with them. It felt good to hold them close. My beret fell off and Casey put it on. It fell over her eyes and nose, the soft cashmere resting on her rosy, little lips. Cole yanked it off her head and pulled it onto his. Casey yelled at him in protest. As I tried my best to maintain the peace, giving each child a chance to wear the beret, I looked up at Dad and saw a big fat tear running down his cheek. This night meant everything to him.

⸙

Janet didn't sit down all evening. She remained in the periphery of the living room behind the couch, moving between that spot and their huge kitchen with the granite countertops. Though there was a smile plastered across her face, I could tell that tonight was painful for her. After all, I had caused her enough grief over the years, constantly pushing her away. I wished I could wash it all away and start anew; show Janet just how nice I could be. We had avoided each other for so long, her reaching out and me responding with silence and disdain, that it was hard to pretend now, even in this happy setting.

The smell of cinnamon and citrus wafted into the living room. Janet was making her delicious sticky buns, the kind where she poured orange glaze on the bottom of the round pan and baked the cinnamon-sugar dough just right. She dumped it over while the delicacy cooled on a wire rack. The result was a sticky, gooey sweet treat that was crispy outside and soft and billowy on the inside. Perfection. I couldn't wait to taste it. Those rolls alone should've made me give her a chance all those years ago.

Then the phone rang.

"It's your mother," said Janet, thrusting the cordless in my direction. "She sounds upset."

I reached over and grabbed the phone. It wasn't odd to hear my mother was mad, but it was unlikely that she would call me here, especially when she was in St. George. She avoided my dad and Janet as much as possible. She acted like their home was full of an infectious disease, as if someone needed to call HAZMAT.

"Mom? Hello?"

"Avery! The baby! Katelyn's baby is coming!"

"Oh my gosh…really? It's time? Did her water break?"

"Yes. She said it gushed like the mountain streams in springtime. Ha! That little baby of hers is well on her way! She says the contractions are steady and hard, now. She's already at the hospital. I'm in the car on my cell phone headed back to Salt Lake. I just talked with Katelyn and she wanted me to tell you to get there as fast as you can."

My mouth dropped open. I couldn't believe it was finally time. The faint cacophony of the kids playing in the wrapping paper with Dad behind me was like a distant home video. The events of this Christmas Eve were already turning into a sepia tone memory. I reached for my keys on the black granite countertop. Janet grabbed my thick, wool coat and handed it to me, a woman who understood the urgency of labor.

"Bye, Casey! Bye, Cole! I gotta run, guys!" I yelled into the next room feeling a strong pang of guilt for leaving early now, and for never having taken any interest in them before. "Thanks for the fun night! Merry Christmas, Dad. My friend is having a baby!"

I didn't wait for their response.

I leapt outside into my clunky car and frantically turned on the defroster. It was pitch black outside except for the twinkling of Janet and Dad's white Christmas lights that lined the doorway. The windshield on my car was an opaque sheet of ice. My heart was pounding in my chest and my breaths were quick and frantic. I felt like I was sweating, though I was freezing from the cold. I made myself take a deep breath and wait for the old defrost to do its work on the windshield so I could see. I'd be no good to

Katelyn if I didn't calm down and think clearly. My fingers felt like icicles. I rubbed them together and dug through my purse for my favorite black gloves. *You can do this, Avery, be strong,* I told myself. *Your friend needs you.*

❧❧❧❧

The smell in labor and delivery was a mixture of hospital ammonia, baby powder and fresh flowers. The wood floors were polished to a high shine. There were neat laundry bales at each corner of the hallway full of soiled bed linens. Nurses in pale pink doctor's scrubs moved about their stations without emotion, as if babies being born happened every day, which of course, it did. A short woman standing next to me appeared as if she was about to tip over from the weight of her pregnant belly. Her husband looked at me blankly, like he was in shock. He stroked his wife's arm without blinking. He was pale. I stepped back realizing they needed help first, but the woman gave me a nod that said they were already being taken care of. She made her mouth into a small "o" as she sucked air in and braced for another contraction. Then she smiled without any fear behind her pretty, green eyes. I looked up at the "checked-in" board full of names, "Abrams, rm. 356; Clark, rm. 311; Christianson, rm. 340; Jamison, rm. 308…"

"Hi. That's—that's my friend, Katelyn Jamison. Room 308. She's having a baby. I need to help her." Had I lost all ability to be articulate? Why was I stating the obvious to these nurses? "I'm her coach," I blurted out.

"You are her coach?" An older, heavyset nurse stared up at me above the gold bifocals perched on her nose. She was scribbling something on her chart. I saw judgment in her eyes and caught a hard glimpse of what Katelyn had been going through for nine, long months now. It struck me that this was only the beginning.

That nurse turned on her heels and headed off in another

direction. I wanted to shout after her, "Mind your own business!" But I figured I better not, we might need her later.

"Her coach, huh, what's your name?" asked a younger, seemingly kinder nurse seated at the counter. Her brown hair was flipped up at the ends and her eyes turned up at the corners.

"I'm Avery Rose."

"Yes, Avery, she's been expecting you. That's not all she's been expecting…"

How could a nurse crack a joke at a time like this? She was so nonchalant, so calm I could hardly believe it. Didn't she know that this was an emergency? Katelyn's big day was here.

"Go ahead to room 308, down the hall, that way," she said sweetly. The nurse pointed down a dark hallway. I numbly put one foot in front of the other and tried to muster courage I was certain I didn't have.

When I found Katelyn sitting up in her hospital bed she was in the middle of a contraction. Her face was writhing with a painful, red-hot expression. She was holding her breath and I knew from the class I took with her that she should be breathing through the pain instead. Her parents were at her side and her mother was holding her hand, looking as if she were feeling her daughter's pain by osmosis. I noticed beads of sweat forming on her dad's forehead. For the first time, I could see how painful all of this was for them, too.

"Deep breaths, Katelyn! Breathe in and out. Breathe through the pain. You can do this," I said, taking her other hand in mine. Katelyn didn't break her concentration. Katelyn's hair was drenched with sweat. She leaned over in the hospital bed and clenched her teeth.

Finally, the contraction subsided and she exhaled with relief.

We all did. She said that the pain was like a wracking, twisting, breaking in her hips.

"I'm so glad you're here. Thank goodness," said Katelyn, looking at me with such trust. "Where in the heck is my epidural? I asked for one a long time ago!"

"I'm sure the anesthesiologist is on his way," I said, though I truly had no idea.

Her dad said, "I'll go see what's taking him so long." And he left the room, appearing grateful to have something to do.

Katelyn's mom held up a long thin paper that came out of one of the machines that was monitoring her contractions. "Now that was a big one, Kate. Look at that!"

"Mom, please. Believe me, I'm well aware of how big it was. I don't want to feel this pain! I can't believe anyone would ever want to do natural childbirth. They're insane. I feel like my hips are breaking in two! I can't do this, Mommy. I can't do this!" She sobbed. It was one of the saddest sights I've seen. She looked like a little girl watching her carefree youth disappear, painfully, before her very eyes. She was too young to feel pain of that magnitude.

"Now hang in there, Katelyn," I offered. "You're doing great." I remembered at the child birth class the teacher said the coach must "always stay positive."

"She's right, Kate," her mom chimed in. "You can do this. No one ever said it was going to be easy." I prayed her mom would not continue along these lines. This was no time to turn the situation into a lesson. Katelyn has had plenty of those, enough to last a lifetime.

"This is so exciting! Your baby is on her way! Can you believe it? This is going to be amazing," I said, forcing a grin. I truly had no idea what I was in for.

"Oh no, here comes another one, oh gosh!" She wrinkled her brow again and clenched her teeth. She disappeared into a silent world of white hot, agonizing pain. Her mom and I held on to her hands while she squeezed them with all of her might. I thought she might break the bones of my fingers, but figured the pain I felt in my fingers was nothing compared to what she was going through. The contraction seemed to last forever. As it started to subside, she let out a moan with her exhalation. It was hard to watch her in this much agony. All I kept thinking was *no way will I ever do this!*

"Where is that epidural? What's taking so long?" Katelyn shrieked. She was desperate.

"Okay, the anesthesiologist is on his way." Katelyn's dad shot in. "And look who's here, Kate?"

A stylish, little woman with a silver bob and ethereal skin amidst her wrinkles, with an equally charming older man on her arm, walked into the expansive labor room. It was Katelyn's Grandma and Grandpa Payton.

Katelyn pushed her black hair away from her face, wiped her tears and then those beautiful baby blue eyes of hers lit up. "Grandma and Grandpa! I'm so glad you are here. You're here."

The sight of Grandma and Grandpa Payton was like a soothing salve to Katelyn's pain.

"Hello, dear. Are you hanging in there okay?" Grandma Payton patted Katelyn's tear-stained cheek. "Honey-pie, you're going to be just fine. I know you're going to sail through this. We love you, sweetheart. With all our hearts, we love you." Grandma Payton's voice was cracking and I could see she was having difficulty suppressing her emotions.

"I love you guys, too."

"Hi pretty girl," said Grandpa Payton. "You gonna have yourself another pretty girl for us to love? Eh?" He turned to me. "She's been convinced that she's having herself a little girl, she won't even consider the possibility that she could have a boy. It's just got to be a girl, right? The women of this family are strong, and usually accurate, so maybe she's right." Grandpa Payton chuckled. Ah, the wisdom and calmness old age can bring.

I reached across Katelyn's pregnant belly and offered Grandma and Grandpa Payton my hands.

"Hello. I'm Avery," I said warmly. "I've heard so much about you both. Let me just say that it is such an honor to--"

"Stop! Everyone quiet!" yelled Katelyn, gasping for breath. "I need everyone quiet! Here's another…" Then she vanished in that deep, dark, paralyzing pain. I looked around the room and saw three generations of agony. They all watched poor Katelyn and their faces writhed with her pain. Grandma Payton whispered something with great concern to Katelyn's parents. I heard her father say in a hushed tone, "Don't worry, the doctor is on his way."

❦

The anesthesiologist made Katelyn curl up into a tiny ball, a nearly anatomically impossible feat considering her pregnant girth. Still, the doctor kept encouraging her to "hug her knees as close as possible" while lying on her side. Then he administered the epidural into her spine. I saw Katelyn jump and her eyes grow wider as he inserted the large needle, even though they had first numbed the skin on her back. I reached for my back and held a pain I was sure I was feeling on her behalf. This looked like a terrifying thing to have to go through. I held her hand and her mom stroked her face. We were all saying prayers that Katelyn would get through this, and that soon she would be holding a healthy baby.

The epidural gave her instant relief. She was herself again. But it also had the undesirable effect of slowing down her labor. While the contractions had been coming between three and four minutes a part, they had slowed to seven to ten minutes now. Her doctor didn't like this at all. He was an older man named Dr. Berkstrom, with bushy white eyebrows and a shiny head surrounded by silver wisps of hair, with a striking likeness to Santa Claus, only he was wearing doctor's greens and a white coat. I wondered how many thousands of babies he had delivered in his lifetime.

He showed up every few hours to check on Katelyn's progress. I had pictured the doctor would be here the whole time, holding her hand with me, coaxing her along. We hardly saw him, to tell the truth. At times, he would check in by phone. As twelve hours stretched into fourteen, Dr. Berkstrom decided to give her some medicine to help speed those contractions back up. He said he didn't want to start talking C-section yet, but it was a possibility looming in the background. Katelyn shuddered each time he mentioned it. I knew how terrified she was of having a surgical birth. The only time she had been under the knife was for a tonsillectomy when she was seven.

<hr />

I'm not sure I've ever been so tired in all of my life. Katelyn, amazingly, was napping. I guess those epidurals really do their job. She had been asleep for about an hour.

It was 11:00 a.m. Christmas Day. I couldn't believe Katelyn had been in labor more than 14 hours. It felt more like 14 days. Grandma and Grandpa Payton were in the waiting room drinking hot chocolate and making conversation with other grandparents-to-be, making sure the others knew they were extra special…great grandparents to be. They both went home for a brief shower that morning, after having stayed up all night with us. They seemed to be handling this whole scenario much better than me.

"Good morning and Merry Christmas!" Portly Dr. Berkstrom walked in. I half expected him to 'wiggle his belly like a bowl full of jelly.' "Sorry to wake you, Katelyn, but we've got to see how you're progressing. We need to get that baby here. Won't it be terrific?

Your baby will be born on Christmas Day! That's so special." He lifted the blanket covering Katelyn's legs to see how her labor was moving forward. As he checked her, he continued talking. "We all take a picture in the lobby Christmas night—the holiday babies and parents, it's a hospital tradition. Free doughnuts, if you're interested."

I stared at him blankly. I don't handle the combination of no sleep and no shower well. I felt icky and out of sorts. The outfit I wore last night that felt so right for the occasion now hung on me in a rumpled, heavy heap. And I needed a toothbrush, desperately. It was almost afternoon and all the junk food I'd had from the vending machines was catching up to me in one nasty aftertaste.

"So, how am I doing?" A groggy Katelyn asked, rubbing her eyes.

"That medicine has done the trick! You are dilated to a ten. You are ready."

Dr. Berkstrom picked up the phone in the labor and delivery room and called for the nurses to join him. How could this be moving so quickly now? In seconds, three nurses appeared in the room and another petite nurse behind them rolled in a little hospital bassinette. My stomach dropped down to my feet. I wrung my hands and shifted my weight. I couldn't help myself. A little person was going to be in that little bed! A real person. All this time, I'd been consumed with concern about Katelyn. "The baby" had always been out there, not real to me at all, more of a concept then an actuality. The reality that a new soul was entering the world, the magnitude of that miracle, and the awesome responsibility made me feel light headed.

The slow silence of the quiet labor room now sped up into fast forward motion. The nurses prepared the bed for the baby and positioned themselves around Katelyn and took orders from Dr. Berkstrom. He got on his stool and wheeled close to her.

At this moment, I was glad "Santa" was such a kind man. He seemed genuine in his excitement, despite the less than ideal circumstances.

Katelyn's mom ran out to get Grandma and Grandpa Payton. Her father paced the delivery room, awkward, unsure of what to do next.

"Now when we see the next contraction come on the monitor, pull your knees to you like you are rowing a boat and push with all your might. All right? Katie? You can do this. Here we go." No one ever called her "Katie." "Old St. Nick" was starting to get on my nerves.

Then, all of the sudden, just as I thought I might faint, I felt an awesome strength overcome me. I found my footing and stepped into position next to Katelyn. I was brave. I was ready for anything. There was nothing I couldn't handle at that moment. It may have been my finest hour.

"You hold Katelyn's knee while she pushes, Avery," said Dr. Berkstrom. "And where's your mom?" He looked around the bustling room.

"Yes, yes. I'm here. I'm here!" Shouted Katelyn's mom.

"You hold her other knee. And take a deep breath. Okay?"

"Okay. I'm ready," her mom said.

The nurse who stood right by Katelyn gave her the instructions. "Now when the contraction comes, I want you to breathe in as much air as you can and then count out as far as possible while you push. So in and then out—one, two, three, four, five—all the way to fifteen or twenty. We need nice long pushes."

"What do you need me to do?" I asked.

"Just encourage her. You're her best friend and coach, right?" barked the nurse.

"Yeah. I am."

The doctor looked at the monitor attached to Katelyn's belly and saw it begin to peak. "All right, now here we go, Mom, grab your daughter's leg. And, Avery, you grab the other and push upward toward her arms." We all breathed in and pushed with her.

The nurse instructed her. "Now breathe in Katie—big breath in, as much air as you can take—and . . . out . . . one, two, three, four, five, six, seven, eight, nine, ten, eleven, twelve." Everyone in the room let out a collective exhale.

"Nice job!" said Dr. Berkstrom. I sure hoped "Santa" knew what he was doing.

Katelyn's face was crimson red. She looked exhausted already. This was going to be a long, arduous process.

It had been exactly one hour since Katelyn started pushing. If Katelyn appeared exhausted before, she looked like she might pass out now. The nurse slipped an oxygen mask on her face. That seemed to help her breathe a little easier in between pushing. None of us wanted to ask the question "What will happen if the baby doesn't come out soon?" We were all painfully aware of how terrified she was of having to have a C-section. That possibility hung over us like a storm cloud.

Pale pink, ruffled valences hung from the windows that opened up to a picturesque view of the Wasatch Mountains. The floors gleamed in the sunlight that was spilling in through the large window and the sheets were crisp and white. Yet, even the nurse who had smiled at us like a cherub from the beginning was starting to furrow her brow with worry.

With the next contraction, Katelyn wrinkled up her face and pushed out with all the force I think she had left. Still nothing. It seemed futile.

"How's the baby doing?" asked Dr. Berkstrom.

"Heart rate looks good. It drops during the contraction, but still remains in normal range," said the nurse. "Shall I get the forceps?"

"Not just yet," smiled the doctor. "Let's give this little gal a little more time to push her baby out herself. No need to worry yet."

"Yet?" Shrieked Katelyn's mom. "How long do you expect her to keep this up, doctor? Can't you do something?"

"Mommy!" Katelyn was crying. "I—I can't do this anymore, Mommy. Please, make it stop! I'm so tired. I need to rest! Mommy!" Though Katelyn was 18, legally an adult, she sounded like she was ten years old.

"Now, now. Stay calm," he said. "This isn't so tough, now is it?" I had the urge to send him back to the North Pole. Though, I had to remind myself that he delivered babies—lots of them—every single day. This was by no means a strenuous experience for him. "The best thing we all can do is not panic," he continued. "Sometimes these babies like to take their sweet time. They make their mommies work for them." Then he winked and left the room to check on his other patients.

I was certainly inexperienced in this arena, but I couldn't help wondering if he was letting Katelyn go way past the usual limit and into danger.

Another hour passed without the baby moving one inch. Katelyn was disappearing into a thick fog of exhaustion and delirium. She could hardly speak to us anymore. Her pushes were growing weaker and weaker. Even her face seemed limp and lifeless while we lifted her knees and encouraged her to push.

Dr. Berkstrom checked on her progress very frequently, but it still didn't seem like enough. I wished he would stay with us.

Her grandma and grandpa peeked in to say "hello" every now and then, rather than staying in the room. They were from an age when childbirth was a very private affair. Not even husbands were allowed in the room. Katelyn told me that Grandpa Payton didn't see even one of five children born. The whole process was kept sterile and isolated, a great mystery. My, how times have changed.

I needed a quick break. I walked down the hall and saw rooms full of happy family members helping the screaming mother along. At the foot of each bed was a devoted husband, sweating it out with his wife. My heart ached for Katelyn that she didn't have that kind of support. It was a noticeable absence.

When I walked back into Katelyn's room the doctor was already there. "All right. What do you say we get that baby of yours out of there? Ready for your Christmas gift, Katie?"

"No, No." Katelyn's face shot to attention, like someone coming back from the dead. "I don't want a C-section. Please doctor, let me keep trying." Tears streamed down her face. She was shaking. "Just a little longer. Please!"

I saw anguish in Katelyn's mom and dad's faces as they weighed every word that the doctor said.

"I don't like how long the baby has been in the birth canal. Soon, his or her heart rate will start to plummet. We don't want to risk that."

"Oh, gosh. No! Mommy, I can't do this, Mommy!" shrieked Katelyn.

"Now don't worry, Katie. We're going to just try to help your baby along a little. That's all." Dr. Berkstrom turned to the nurses. "Instruments, please."

"Here we go, Katie. You won't feel a thing. Let's just wait for another contraction. Here we go. I see you're starting one. Everyone into position." He sounded calm. And then it all happened so fast. Seconds later—the top of a tiny head of dark, curly hair appeared, just a peek, but the baby didn't budge any further. "All right, I've got the shoulders. Big push, Katie. Push with all your might!"

"You can do this, Katelyn. You're almost there. I—I love you

Katelyn! You're about to see your baby!" I shouted, surprising myself.

"I feel like I'm going to pass out," Katelyn said weakly.

Dr. Berkstrom shot back, "Her blood pressure is dropping. Let's get this baby out, now!" He sounded panicked for the first time. I didn't like what I was hearing one bit. I felt a prickly sensation go down my spine. Dr. Berkstrom barked up in her direction: "Just hang on there, Katie, as soon as your baby's out you'll feel better, immediately. Now push. With all your might."

"Come on Katelyn, push, push, push," coaxed her mother.

"Push again, Katelyn. You're almost there!" I screamed.

Katelyn was grunting and breathing hard. Her gorgeous dark hair was wet with sweat. Poor Katelyn looked so pitiful there all pale, nearly translucent and weak with an oxygen mask over her nose and mouth. The minutes seemed liked hours.

Just when I thought she was going to give up, she let out a loud moan, one final push of strength when there seemed to be no energy left.

Out came one perfect little girl with jet-black curly hair, milky skin, and soft, round features, all covered in a pasty white film. I will never forget that moment. After a long minute of tenuous silence, the infant cried with surprising potency. This tiny angel emanated strength in her perfection.

Katelyn craned her neck to get a look at her. Her mom and dad were crying. I was bawling. The nurses placed her on Katelyn's stomach while the doctor cut the umbilical cord. I learned from the birthing course we took that the baby's father usually did that. I felt a small pang of sadness again for Katelyn, but pushed it away. This was a glorious day.

Katelyn reached down and touched her daughter's head. The second her fingers brushed her infant, the baby quieted and looked up toward her mother in an amazing moment of connection. It was as if the baby was saying, "I know you."

"Hi, Payton," Katelyn's voice was shaky from crying tears of pure joy. "I'm your momma. And I love you. Love you forever honey, it's just you and me."

Then she took a deep breath and looked up at her parents with tears filling her eyes, her brow wrinkled with anguish. "I can't do it. I can't give her up. I'm sorry. She's staying with me."

Katelyn's mother and father began to weep but it was unclear if it was because of joy, sadness, or relief that it was over—maybe a combination of all three.

All my muscles relaxed with relief. She did it. The baby was finally here. We were high as the fluffy clouds in the clear-blue Christmas day sky. But like threatening rain, other thoughts hovered over that happy moment. I couldn't help thinking of the Carters, Mal's contagious smile and Buddy's endearing honesty, and how devastated they would be when they learned they wouldn't become parents this time around. They'd have to wait even longer, still, for their dreams to come true.

> *Dear Lucrezia,*
> *This is the day that Payton Avery Jamison was born.*
> *I'm changed forever after witnessing her birth. My outlook on life is completely different. I can't help but think that everybody is somebody's baby.*
> *Payton has perfect pink lips and tiny rounded knees. Her little feet are as delicate as a rose. How could my mother, who surely must have looked at me like that with so much love, years later, speak to me with so many painful insults? How could she have made so many mistakes in my life?*
> *And yet, at the same time, something tells me that mothers and fathers do the best that they know how. No one sets out to mess up her child's life. They do their darnedest given their circumstances.*

I guess this is another good reason to "hold to the iron rod" and keep the faith like the scriptures tell us. It can be our roadmap, our guide, through murky waters.
Avery

11

Pale yellow sunlight spilled into Katelyn's room in the maternity ward. I had such a feeling of peace. I sat in the cozy hospital chair, holding warm, little Payton in my arms while Katelyn snoozed in the bed next to me. With my pointer finger, I stroked Payton's tiny, round palm and she immediately grabbed a tight hold. I brushed her petal soft cheek. She looked straight into my eyes, appearing to be so wise, so knowing. How could this be?

I felt unabashed happiness. Though I was still exhausted and a little sore from straining my muscles right along with Katelyn, I had gotten a good night's sleep at home last night.

The frightened child in labor just the day before was no more. She was blossoming into a young mother, as if she was filling out into her mother's pair of elegant dress shoes. Her pale skin was smooth and clear. Her dark hair was freshly washed, shiny and thick, falling in loose curls around her face.

There were tough times to come, no doubt. The difficulties of raising a child without a husband at such a young age, I'm sure she couldn't fully comprehend. I'm sure she grieved her grave sin, so blatant to the world, and wished she had brought Payton into better circumstances.

But for now, Katelyn was full of relief and true love like she had never known.

A middle-aged nurse with jet-black hair cut in a neat bob

pushed the door open into the room, slicing the serene moment. She wore yellow scrubs cinched at her bulging waist and didn't look up from her clipboard. Her entry was so obtrusive it immediately woke Katelyn with a startle.

"Where's the baby's father?" The nurse barked. "We need him to sign some paternity papers." She rested her paperwork on her hip and stared menacingly into Katelyn's innocent eyes.

"Ugh, Logan? He's not in the picture at all anymore." Katelyn was groggy. She yawned and rubbed her eyes, trying to bring herself back to consciousness. "I don't even know where he is right now, to tell you the truth."

"You don't even know where he is?" The nurse shifted her weight and shook her head, trying to take in the serious nature of what she had just learned. "You need to find out. If he's relinquishing paternity rights he needs to make it legal. You know, 'sign the dotted line.'" With exaggeration, she signed the stuffy air with her right hand.

I felt the sudden urge to protect Payton from this judgmental woman. I held the sleeping infant closer to my chest and stroked her face. The only thing that kept me from screaming at the nurse was the fact that I didn't want to upset the precious baby I held in my arms.

"Excuse me," I said, forcing politeness into my voice. "It's not Katelyn's fault that her boyfriend has been absent in this situation. He ducked out, not Katelyn. Please don't use that tone with her." My voice was measured and cool. I looked directly into the nurse's beady eyes that were flanked by long, dark lashes. There was a faint scar on her left cheek. "With all due respect, this young woman has had more courage in the last nine months than you probably have had in your whole lifetime."

She pursed her lips. "Just find the baby's father," she spoke slowly. I could tell she was using all the self-control she could muster; remembering what they taught her in "conflict resolution training" at the last hospital seminar. "We can fax him the forms if we have to," adopting a lighter tone, without making eye contact with either one of us. Then she turned and left the room as quickly as if it had caught fire.

Katelyn looked at me with tears in her eyes. "Well, that was rude," she said.

"Totally." I answered. "Don't even give her the pleasure of knowing she made you feel bad. People like that are just angry; angry at the whole world and they've got to take it out on someone. It shouldn't be you." I patted her arm.

"Thanks, Avery, for what you said to her. I want you to know how much I appreciate what an..." Katelyn's voice caught in her throat. "Amazing friend you have been. I will always be grateful. You pulled me through this, you know? You really did. I never thought I could've made it through, I'm sure I couldn't have without you."

"You know," I answered. "I've never had a best friend like you before. I mean, I've always had Barclay. But that's different—and so weird and messed up now. I don't know what I'm going to do about that." I leaned down and kissed baby Payton's downy soft head. She smelled strangely sweet. "Now I have two best girlfriends, though. Who could ask for more than that?"

Katelyn smiled, showing her pearly white teeth, revealing a slight overbite I'd never noticed before. Somehow, it only made her prettier. "I feel pretty lucky. Now hand me my baby. My baby, it still sounds so strange to say that. Strange in the most wonderful way."

I put Payton in her proud mother's arms. A calmness and serenity stretched across Katelyn's face as she held Payton.

"Knock, knock." My mom peeked around the hospital door. She was holding a large vase full of pink carnations. Her blond hair was styled smooth around her tastefully made up face. She wore a chunky navy turtleneck sweater and matching stretch pants.

"Hel-lo . . ." Grams appeared behind Mom. "How's the new mama?" Grams had a ridiculous silver theme going on today. She had on a silver quilted jump suit with a dark gray sash. Her white hair was in tight curls around her head. Her puffy, white winter vest had metallic silver on the seams. Heavy, silver teardrop earrings hung from her sagging lobes. She wore ankle boots the color of a new nickel. She looked like an ill-equipped senior citizen astronaut headed to the moon.

Mom went straight for baby Payton. Years peeled off her as she picked up the infant and cradled her, spoke to her in cooing tones. She appeared to be looking back in time.

"So how did it go? The birth?" asked Grams. "Did you have to have stitches? That's the worst part of the whole thing in my oh-pinion. It isn't exactly a picnic now, is it." Grams stood at the foot of the bed with her arms folded. She always had been direct and to-the-point.

Katelyn said, "Yeah, but I'm feeling no pain thanks to the medicine they gave me. And I'm just so glad that I didn't have to have a C-section." Katelyn looked Grams up and down. Her jaw dropped. She quickly snapped it back together, finding a pleasant expression, before Grams noticed.

"That's good, dear. Now do you plan to nurse or bottle feed her?" Grams scooted closer to Katelyn and I decided it was time to intervene a bit.

"Grams—it's nice of you to come, but I'm sure you understand that Katelyn is very exhausted right now. She probably shouldn't be answering a lot of questions."

"But I just want to know—"

"Now, Mom," interjected my mother. "Let her be. Just let her be. She's got a lot on her plate right now. Don't push things. 'A watched pot never boils.' We need to ease into it. Let things unfold, all right."

What was my mom talking about? It was looking like she and

Grams had formulated some sort of plan.

"Ease into what, Mom?" My tone was guarded.

"Oh now, Avie. Please. Don't always assume the worst." Though Mom was speaking to me, she directed her comments at Katelyn, with a grin as genuine as cubic zirconium. "She's always done that—make 'mountains out of mole hills.'"

"Mom. What's going on? What are you trying to say?" I held my breath and tried to calm my rapidly beating heart. I looked at Katelyn, and she remained serene and groggy. Must have been all those painkillers they had given her. Her eyelids looked heavy.

"Just ask her. I think it's good to get it out there. Go on now," said Grams, tapping one metallic foot.

Mom took a deep breath. She stood up and returned Payton to Katelyn's arms. "I've been thinking about this for some time. I must say that it's been downright inspiring seeing the friendship you and Avery have formed. You two were so different in high school. I never could have dreamed then that you'd one day become such dear friends." Mom's laugh was nervous and false.

"Anyway, I know things are not great with your parents, Katelyn. It's been tough on all of you. I just wanted to extend the offer for you and the baby to stay with us. On I Street. Until you get back on your feet."

There it was. My mouth dropped open. My mother was doing the most selfless act I had ever witnessed her do. What's more, Grams was nodding her head in approval and smiling, like she had encouraged the whole idea.

"You would do that, Ms. Rose? For us?"

"Ah, call me Margaret. Please—especially if we're going to be housemates. And yes, I'm serious about this offer."

I was dumbfounded. A big grin stretched across Katelyn's tired face. She looked back at my mother like that was the most natural proposition ever. I, on the other hand, knew what a big deal it was for my mother to be so incredibly unselfish and kind.

Or, maybe she'd always had it in her and I'd just never been able to see it.

But what would Katelyn think of the monster couch? How well would she and the baby fare around all my mother's stacks of stuff? I was self-conscious yet tried to remind myself that those things didn't really matter. Still, I formed a plan to buy a tasteful slipcover to tame the sofa before Katelyn and Payton came home from the hospital.

"We would love to! That sounds just perfect! Thank you. Thank you all so much!" Katelyn looked down at her baby girl who had just woken up. "It sounds just great. Doesn't it, sweet pea? Do you want to go live with your Aunt Avery and me? Yes. What do you think?" Payton peered back at her mother with her glossy little ovals. The baby's movements were slow and graceful. Her downy, dark hair stuck up every which way. She was a luminous sight, even if she did seem to take after Logan. It struck me then that Katelyn was going to have a 24-7 reminder of the guy who left her.

But there in that peachy-pink hospital room with the warm glow from the sun, surrounded by three stubborn women who loved her, somehow, it would all work out. I knew the two of them were going to be just fine.

Katelyn's warm smile gave way to a scowl. "How are we going to convince my mom of this plan? They're going to be upset. My mom and dad are never going to go for this." Katelyn looked over at me, furrowing her brow. "I feel a battle coming on, not sure I'm up for it."

"Just talk to them when they get back from showering," I offered. "I'm sure they'll want what is best for the both of you."

"Heck!" Grams interjected, clicking her long, fake fingernails on the metal part of the hospital bed. "You're an adult. Technically, you can make your own decisions. Not only an adult, you're a momma, too. You got to start thinking of your child first, what's best for her." Grams folded her arms in triumph.

I could see what Papa had said about Grams' strong will coming in handy at times. If only we could learn to temper her. It's hard to come to terms with the fact that she's not going to live forever. She seems so strong, so invincible, with a character larger than life—too huge to contain most of the time. With all of her flamboyance and spice, I couldn't imagine life being nearly as interesting without Grams.

"You're right," said Katelyn. There was a resolute tone in her voice. "Payton and I are taking you up on your offer. I hope Mom and Dad will be supportive."

❧❧❧

I went for hot chocolate from the hospital cafeteria, hoping they had cinnamon available. Then I saw that slouchy walk and mop of brown hair that I know so well heading tentatively toward me. Barclay's hands were in his pockets and I knew he was probably weary of this moment. We hadn't really defined our relationship since the kiss. How nice of him to visit Katelyn and the baby, I thought. I could always count on Barclay.

"Hey," he said while studying the glossy floor.

"Hey, Barc! How are you?" I asked, with too much nervous enthusiasm.

"Um, good. I guess. You?"

"Great. Never better, actually. Wait until you see Payton. She's beautiful. Amazing, really. She has tons of dark hair. Katelyn named her after her grandparents, the really nice ones. And her middle name is Avery. What an honor."

"Yeah. I'll say. And how's Katelyn?"

"Really well, it seems. She already seems like a natural to me. I guess she's going to come and live with us for a while, with the baby."

"Really? Your mom went for that plan?"

"She actually suggested it."

"You're kidding." Barclay looked up at me and shook the hair out of his eyes in one jerking motion. How I adored those hazel, puppy dog eyes of his.

"No, I'm not kidding. I guess sometimes people can surprise you, even your parents." At the word 'parents' I winced, thinking maybe I shouldn't have brought them up around Barclay. He was still trying desperately to recover from his mother's death.

"Hey, don't worry about it."

"I—I'm sorry Barclay. That was so insensitive of me. Here I am complaining and . . ."

"Avie, please don't apologize. I'm doing all right." Barclay looked down again, and then off down the hallway.

"How was your Christmas?" I asked, changing the subject.

"Ah, it was bad. My dad's never been one for festivities. I went to Ruth's Diner for dinner by myself. Good food, but it still was depressing."

"I'm sorry, Barc. You could've come here."

"I didn't want to interfere. Anyway, it sounds like you had everything under control. Hey, I have a belated Christmas present for you."

"You do? Gosh, I'm such a dummy. I haven't even been thinking about Christmas I've been so focused on the birth. I'm sorry."

"Stop apologizing. Just show up at West High one month from tonight at 7:00 p.m. All right? Will you be there? I'm telling you now so you can put it on your calendar. I'll be flying back from MIT for the weekend."

"The high school? Why?" I squinted at him. "What are you up to? Why are you flying here for just a couple of days?"

"It's a surprise. Promise me you'll come?"

"I'll be there, Barclay."

"I better head down to see Payton. Do you think she'll like this?" Barclay pulled the most ridiculous stuffed animal I'd ever seen out of his book bag. It was a bright purple elephant wearing a hot pink tutu and tomato red ballerina slippers. The elephant's snout was so long it reached the tip of its loud, satiny feet.

"It's perfect. She'll love it. Want some hot chocolate? I'm headed to the cafeteria to get some for everyone."

"Nah, I'm good. I'm great, actually, thanks." Barclay's smile was brighter than I'd seen in a long time. "Don't forget the cinnamon." I continued down the corridor wondering what Barclay could be planning for me. I'd never liked surprises.

Dear Lucrezia,

It's funny, you know. I used to look at Katelyn with her parents at church and envy them. They always seemed like the "perfect family." I know that Katelyn isn't abandoning them, no matter what they might think. She just needs to step out for a while and feel like she's on her own in some way. That's what we're doing for her. I'm going to say a little prayer for all of them tonight.

I'm really nervous for next month's surprise. Barclay says it's my belated Christmas present. I'm a little terrified he's done something crazy like gone and bought a wedding ring.

It's difficult to sort out my feelings for him. The thought of him being my boyfriend terrifies me for some reason. But, when I saw Barclay with his slouchy walk, in the hallway at the hospital, my heart started pounding in my chest. I felt warmth wash over me, like Barclay always makes everything all right.

I wonder what a great beauty like you would do in my shoes? If only you lived today and we could become friends. Wish me luck. I'll need it.

Avery

12

The baby would be one month old today. It was 4:00 a.m. and Payton had worked herself into a frenzy of crying. It sounded like she might never stop. It was so abrupt to hear such strident screaming in the dark silence of the wee hours of the morning. I found Katelyn looking haggard in her robe pacing in the kitchen, bouncing her fussy baby girl in her arms. Katelyn was sobbing with frustration, desperately trying to wipe the tears that were rolling down her cheeks.

"Nothing is working," she said with a wrinkled brow and a deep frown. There were puffy bags under her eyes.

The house was a complete mess. It was a pitiful sight. Tigger flounced into the room and then lowered her tail and ears. She must have sensed the stress because she turned right around and went back into my bedroom to sleep.

"Looks rough," I shouted over Payton's screams. "How can I help?"

"I don't know what to do! I've tried everything," cried Katelyn. She was doing deep knee bends trying to soothe Payton. "I've nursed her, I've tried the binkie, I changed her diaper—nothing's working! Not even the bouncy seat, that's usually a sure thing! I don't know what's wrong!" Her voice was a frantic shriek.

Then, Katelyn's eyes became morose. Her voice was full of fear. "What if something is terribly wrong with her?" she said.

"Where's the pediatrician's number?"

She fiddled through the stacks of stuff for the phone number. It was futile. Finding anything in all those old piles of mail, magazines and newspapers would take a major excavation. Even Columbus would've steered away from exploring the Rose family kitchen.

Katelyn's blood-shot eyes flashed back and forth. She shifted Payton again, this time to a gentle rocking position in the crook of her arm. But the baby's cries were now a high-pitched scream that turned her whole little face purplish red.

"I've got to call now—or maybe I should just call 9-1-1." Complete panic enveloped Katelyn. "Where's the phone? I can't find anything around here! It's such a mess!"

I put my arms out, and pled with my eyes for Katelyn to hand Payton over so I could try to calm her down. As I cradled Payton's fragile neck and lifted her into my arms, her screaming toned down a notch to an angry, throaty gurgle. She eased into a self-calming cooing and began sucking her fingers. Her color slowly resumed to its normal peachy-pink. The storm was over.

Katelyn teetered on the edge of a wooden chair across from us trying to avoid the piles that rested in a delicate balance behind her. I looked up and smiled, expecting to see gratitude in her expression. Instead, I saw cold, hard rage.

"Sometimes it just takes some fresh arms; just a little change can calm them right down, at least that's what my mom says," I offered.

"I'm not cut out for this." Katelyn said in a shouting whisper. "I don't know what I was thinking, Avery, that I could handle this. Well, I can't. She doesn't even want me. Already I'm messing up. She doesn't even want me. She wants you instead. You're not even family. We're just your stupid charity case."

Ouch. That one hurt. I couldn't believe what I was hearing. Where was this coming from? After all I'd done for her, how ungrateful. I felt the steamy hot feeling of anger rising up deep inside of me. The soft feeling of Payton sleeping in my arms doused my fire.

"It's not that she wants me instead of you. She just needed fresh arms for a minute, that's all. She can't tell us what's wrong—maybe nothing's wrong. It seems to be a guessing game with infants. I suppose that I just happened to guess right this time. You've already guessed right a hundred times before." I looked up at her and remembered how incredibly overwhelmed she must've been feeling. "And you're going to guess correctly a million times more in the future. You'll make mistakes, Katelyn. All moms do. I guess it's inevitable. But you stick with her, try harder and love her."

"You think? Really?" Katelyn sniffed.

"Yeah, of course. This baby has a mom who loves her more than anything. She's fortunate."

"Right, real fortunate," said Katelyn, rolling her eyes.

"She is because she has you. And you're lucky to have her."

"I know. I just never imagined it would be this crazy hard. I feel like I've aged a decade in the last month. I mean look at me."

She did look pitiful sitting there in her robe, her hair greasy at the roots and her face, ashen.

"Hang in there. It's going to get easier, at least I hope it will," I winced.

Katelyn let out a nervous laugh.

I continued, "You're exhausted. It's hard to think clearly when you're this tired. Have you been up with her all night?"

"Pretty much." Katelyn rested her elbows on her knees and let her head fall down in her hands. Her hair cascaded down around her shoulders and spilled onto her back.

"Let me stay here with Payton," I whispered. "You go back to bed. She needs you to be rested later."

"No—I want to take her."

"Katelyn, it's the best thing you can do for her right now. When you take care of you, you're also taking care of her."

When did I become so wise?

Katelyn got up and kissed Payton tenderly on the forehead. Then she stroked her little head and opened her mouth to speak but could not. Katelyn was silent, like someone overcome with emotion. While staring at her baby, tears streamed down her face, and her shoulders shook.

"What is it Katelyn? Are you okay?"

She was quiet there for a long time, caressing her baby's delicate temples, pursing her lips together and wiping the tears from her cheeks, a flood of emotion in her eyes.

"You're scaring me, Katelyn," I said, terrified. "Please tell me what's going on."

She whimpered and her voice trembled as she spoke. "Call—Mrs.—Lundhausen—in—the—morning. Let her know," Katelyn's shoulders heaved. "Let her know that the Carter's have a beautiful baby girl." Then she turned away and buried her face in her hands and her shoulders quaked with the weight of what she'd just said.

"Are you sure?" I asked, full of surprise. I never thought she'd be able to do this. "You're exhausted, Katelyn. There's no way you can think clearly now. Let's talk more in the morning."

"No. I've been praying all night long. I didn't want this to be the answer God gave me, but it is. There's no denying it. The Carters are supposed to be Payton's parents. I—I have to give her up."

Katelyn wiped her wet cheeks with her hands, took a deep breath and continued. "Give her back to me for now. I'm going to hold her every second that I can, every single second. She's not leaving my arms until the Carters get here. I don't ever want to forget this night as long as I live. I want the memory of her soft and warm in my arms to carry me through a lifetime."

She disappeared into the quiet darkness of the guest bedroom with Payton in her arms. I heard the door click behind her. I lay my head back on the huge cushions of the monster couch and let it envelope me. I was impressed by her strength and maturity. I felt a sense of dread for the morning to come. When daylight broke, I'd have to call Mrs. Lundhausen with the news. I smiled when I thought about the Carters, probably asleep in their warm comfortable beds, unaware that in the morning they would become parents. Yes, in the morning Buddy and Mallory's dream would come true. I winced too, when I thought of the open wound Payton's absence would leave in Katelyn's heart.

The Carters had agreed to an open adoption, allowing Katelyn to see her daughter as often as they felt appropriate. That had to ease her pain. Still, it was going to be a painful day and I needed all the rest I could get. I prayed for sleep that never came.

It took just one hour from the time I called Mrs. Lundhausen for her to arrive at our house with the Carters. I did my best to straighten up the stacks of stuff. My mom had hurried off to work in a rush that morning. She couldn't take any more time off work. She cried and kissed baby Payton good-bye. Mom looked at me with blood-shot eyes and mouthed the words *I love you.*

The Carters pulled up in a red SUV behind Mrs. Lundhausen's car. They were dressed more casually and thrown together than they were before. Mal had on caramel-colored sweat pants that off set her honey-blond hair that was tied back in a ponytail. Buddy wore a red hooded sweatshirt, jeans and had faint stubble on his unshaven face. They clung to each other as they hurried up the walk, both smiling wide grins and wiping tears from their cheeks.

Mrs. Lundhausen wore a black pant suit and her hair pulled back in a tight bun. She was carrying a stack of papers. She walked at a normal pace behind the Carters, like a nanny enduring two ecstatic kids running circles around her. Her worry lines looked less pronounced and there was a slight spring in her step that was barely noticeable.

After the initial greetings and niceties, Katelyn insisted that I go into the guest room. I tried to convince her that she needed me to be there for moral support during such a monumental moment. But she was stoic. "This is something I have to do by myself, Avery. Just me, Payton, the Carters and God."

So I followed her wishes and stayed in the guest room, pacing nervously around Katelyn's suitcases and the disheveled mess of bottles and burping cloths from the difficult night. I could hear the low hum of voices in the living room, then crying and sobbing. It was all I could do not to run out there to comfort her. But I promised I'd let her do this ominous thing by herself. About a half hour later I heard the front door close and then it was silent. I ran out into the living room and parted the thick curtains.

Katelyn looked angelic in her Sunday best, rocking Payton and holding her close to her heart while standing next to the Carters and Mrs. Lundhausen. Her eyes were shut tightly and her lips were pursed together as she gently bounced her baby. Then, she slowly held her infant out before her, leaned down and put her face next to her baby's cheek and remained there for several minutes. The Carters waited patiently and wept. Tears streamed down Mallory's face. She bit her lip and watched Katelyn with intense focus. Then, Katelyn stretched out her arms, holding Payton toward Mal, the Carters stretched out their arms and received their baby. Mallory's face wrinkled up like someone who couldn't believe the bounty before her. Buddy leaned down and gently kissed Payton's face, then kissed his wife and hugged Katelyn with all his might. His face was red and his shoulders were heaving.

It seemed to take forever for the Carters to put Payton in the car seat in their SUV. Katelyn looked too thin for a woman who gave birth only a month before. She stood with her arms folded tightly watching the Carters. She gasped for breath in between choking sobs. I ran out to the curb and wrapped my arms around my friend. Her tears soaked her blouse and sweater. Her face was pale and her hands were frigid. She couldn't talk for a long time. We stood there in silence, my arm around Katelyn's quaking shoulders, as the Carters blew Katelyn kisses from the SUV, waved frantically and slowly pulled away. They drove down I Street and just like that they were gone. I wondered how Katelyn would recover from this loss.

I turned to walk back up the sidewalk and realized Katelyn wasn't following behind me.

"I can't—go—inside just yet," she said, her voice trembling and her blood-shot eyes full of pain. Katelyn was shaking her hands out nervously, as if she didn't know what to do with them now that Payton was gone. She sat down on the curb and rocked back and forth, back and forth, back and forth. I kept thinking love and loss, love and loss, love and loss. It's the cadence of women, the sad rhythm of life that Katelyn experienced too soon. I sat down next to her on the icy curb, shivered, and studied the lonely street.

After a long while she turned to me, her lips quivering. "They're naming her Kathryn Payton Carter," she said. I took a hold of Katelyn's hand. She smiled, her eyes sparkled and she squeezed my hand back. Then fat tears fell down her face, releasing her agony.

"That's wonderful," I told her. "When will you get to see her next?"

"In a week," she said staring off into the distance. "Seven days have never seemed so long or so far away."

Somehow the night seems blacker when it's below freezing outside. On this night, it was like onyx. My breath was a thin, white cloud in front of my chattering lips. I pulled my coat tighter around me. I ambled up the dilapidated, concrete steps of West High School, the very same ones I had hopped up daily without a second thought for four painful years. It was so eerily quiet around this place that used to be such a bustling part of my life. It was strange to see it so silent and still, much like a bear hibernating. The whole school appeared spooky in the dark, macabre, as if schools are only supposed to exist in the bright light of day.

I wasn't sure now if my teeth were trembling from the cold or from fright. The large brick building loomed in front of me like an omen. I forced the disturbing thoughts out of my head, reassuring myself that, after all, this was Barclay I was meeting. He was goodness to me, though I knew he had a dark side. I moved forward, but what I really wanted to do was turn around and run back to my clunky car and speed back to my warm little house on I Street. But a promise was a promise.

I stepped closer. There was a small, square note taped to the large heavy front doors. In red, thick block lettering it read: "Hi, Avery. Head toward the gym. Barclay."

The note was so cryptic. What was this all about? I opened the door to the foyer and walked past all the trophy cases, making note that I had not contributed a single one of them. The hallways were as black as the night. I could find the rows of metal lockers against the walls in the obscurity. Memories played in my head like a home video, Mrs. Johnson's social studies class, Señor Bell's Spanish class. Walking alone to class while cliques of popular girls passed by me, walking arm in arm laughing together. Hunky boys averted their eyes when they saw me. Katelyn was once a part of that coveted group.

When I got to the double doors that opened up to the gym, there was another, equally vague note scribbled in Barclay's bold lettering: "Enter here, Avery Rose."

My hands were shaking as I lifted them to push through the doors. As I entered into to the high school gym, with its signature musty smell mixed with the scent of polished wood, a draft of warm air enveloped me.

Stunning. That's the best way I can describe what I saw. Brilliant red stars outlined in silver and gold glitter in every shape and size hung from the ceiling. Some low, some high, some perfectly symmetrical, others jagged and unruly, together forming a perfect constellation. A disco ball hung from the center of the gym and threw flecks of dancing light on the dimly lit walls and the hardwood floors as it spun. Helium-filled balloons were everywhere, monochromatic red with fire-engine red ribbons. Even more of them were tied to chairs that surrounded the dance floor. It looked like a nighttime carnival.

As I walked toward Barclay, balloons drifted by at my feet. He was standing in the distance looking dapper in his classic black and white tuxedo. I heard every word of Lee Ann Womack's inspiring melody that was playing on the stereo as I stepped closer to him.

I hope you never fear those mountains in the distance.
Never settle for the path of least resistance.
Promise me that you'll give faith a fighting chance.
And when you get the chance, to sit it out or dance,
I hope you dance. I hope you dance.

I continued walking toward Barclay. He was my lifelong friend, my playmate. But things were changing and I was terrified. He looked so handsome standing straight and tall in his tux.

"Welcome to your prom, Avery. I know that you missed out

in high school and it has always bugged you. So I thought I could make it up to you now," he said, straightening his bow tie.

I'd never seen Barclay so starched or standing so tall in black patent leather dress shoes. I was trembling.

"This is your personal prom."

"You did all this? For me?" I squeaked. Why was it so hard for me to speak?

"Of course I did," he said, as if it were the most ordinary night in the world. "Isn't it great?" He waved his arm around the glittering gymnasium, letting me take it all in. Then he continued, "Now, you can't exactly dance at your prom in your favorite old sweater. So…" I looked down and noticed how plain I looked against this over-the-top setting. Barclay walked over to the stage and jumped up in one fluid movement.

He darted behind the curtain. When he returned he was carrying the most beautiful gown I'd ever seen. "I got you this. I know you like red, that's why I made everything a nice shade of crimson—to heck with what your mother says about it clashing with your hair."

He leaned over and put out his hand. With all the gallantry of a knight, he helped me up onto the stage. I caressed the delicate fabric with my fingers. The dress was a satin scarlet with cap sleeves, scoop neck and a princess waist. It was full and glorious all the way to the ground. The sheen of the fabric caught the light just so, giving the effect that the gown glowed.

"How did you do all of this? I mean, how did you pull this off, Barc?"

"Well, Katelyn gave me some tips on finding the dress and your mom told me your size. I had to jump through quite a few hoops with the old administration to get them to let me use the gym for a night. I guess they thought I was pretty much the 'class weirdo' or something around here. They thought I was going to do something destructive at first. But, then I showed them my

MIT report card and that helped. They were pretty impressed. Oh, and Grams. Can't forget her influence."

"My grandmother had something to do with this?" I asked. Good ol' Grams. "I don't think many people can say no to her."

I held the dress on its hanger over his shoulder while I embraced Barclay. We danced with clumsy feet to the music. He smelled like fresh mint, pine, and a touch of rain. His new bulk from a semester and then some at MIT made him feel strong, different from my shy friend. His arms around me made me feel like he could shelter me from the whole world. I rested my head on his sturdy shoulder. His cheek was smooth shaven, his hair slicked back, all except for that stubborn curly lock that fell in his eyes. Those eyes.

A few recessed lights in the ceiling caught the magic of the disco ball and illuminated it into a million scattered strands of light around us. The cardboard stars hanging from the ceiling turned in and out, making little half circles in the air, reflecting light from their glittered edges. It was comfortably warm in there and the serene stillness emanated through the expansive room. There were basketball hoops at each corner where Barclay had put red balloons, but for all I knew, I was in a palace paved with gold.

I couldn't believe he'd gone to so much effort for me. Especially someone who knew me so well and knew all my flaws. And to recreate a moment that was the source of so much sadness and regret from my past, and turn it into something beautiful, I was beyond words. When the song ended, Barclay looked into my eyes with those adorable hazel windows of his. I could get lost in there.

"Go change, Avie. I can't wait to see you in this. The girls' dressing room is unlocked."

"Barclay, this is the best present anyone has ever given me. I don't know what to say."

"Just go get dressed. And then dance with me, Avery. Like the song says."

I slipped the dress on in the dressing room. I was so grateful that it fit me. It fell around my hips comfortably. If it hadn't, that could have really spoiled the moment.

I'd loathed this dressing room in high school. I dreaded gym class because you had to dress in front of everyone, no private curtained off areas. I was mortified, certain that the popular girls were staring at my fat rolls. I tried to jump into my clothes as quickly as possible, avoiding the chance that someone might sneak an unsightly peek. Usually my clothes would stick to me for the next few hours because I wouldn't even towel off completely, desperate to get covered again.

But those memories faded away as I stared into the big mirror on the concrete wall. I felt like I had made such a metamorphosis into a lady. I hardly recognized the person looking back at me in the smoky mirror. With the satin gown on, I spun around, craning my neck to see what I looked like as the rich fabric elegantly swished around me with my movement. The scoop neck highlighted my silky, pale skin and the cap sleeves were flattering to my arms. The princess waist accented my full, well-proportioned curves. The red dress made my hair look like it was on fire as it spilled in soft wisps onto my shoulders and back. My high forehead appeared regal. My thin eyebrows with their high arches made me look like an old-fashioned movie star. The small cleft of my chin and thin lips looked demure. I could've been straight out of a 1950s film classic. I liked what I saw.

Barclay and I danced all evening in that old gymnasium lit up by a million cardboard stars. It was the most magical evening of my life. *You are so beautiful and so strong*, the kind words my mother had said sounded in my ears. And Barclay's loving revelation a few weeks before: *It's you, Avery, it's always been you.* I thought about the miracle of Payton's birth. What a gift she was, even through all the hardship. I marveled at Katelyn's strength. Because of her courage and sacrifice, Payton would bless the Carters' lives for all eternity. Through the terms of the open adoption, my friend would still always be an integral part of her baby's life. I felt changed forever by that experience and by helping Katelyn, being a true friend to someone who was lonely and afraid, just like I'd been for so long.

What a year it had been. It all started with Italy, confronting a ghost on canvas in order to find the woman I'd become.

That Sunday at church I had so much to be thankful for. As we sang *Joy to the World,* I reflected on the amazing life I had. It was amazing to have experienced the sweetness that that little baby brought to our house, a new serenity and contentment. My mom said that she'd forgotten how a baby brings people into the wonderful present. "When you're holding an infant, you feel immediately happy in the moment," she said. "You celebrate the joy of this new little soul, rather than obsessing over the next chore, the next errand, another day of work. You don't think about the future. You're in the moment."

Thanks to Kathryn Payton Carter, my mother and I are more careful about how we speak to one another. Watching Katelyn grieve over giving her baby up for adoption made me realize how precious the mother-daughter relationship is. It gave me empathy for my own mother. I realized she did the best she could for me, given her circumstances. Most mothers do. The love had always been there. There's no greater power than love.

Though Katelyn's pregnancy was devastating, her baby truly was a gift. She confided in me that before I called her that first time, she had thought about suicide, just ending it all. Katelyn was starting to get over letting go of her daughter. Just yesterday, she received a letter of gratitude in the mail from the Carters with a picture of baby Kathryn in the prettiest pink dress and booties you ever saw. On the back of the photo one of them had written: "Kathryn Payton Carter on her blessing day." I read the letter.

> *Dearest Katelyn,*
> *Kathryn smiled today for the first time, a lovely toothless grin. We wept.*
> *Please know that we are giving Kathryn all the love within our hearts. And, she'll always know what a fine, courageous woman her birth mother is and that you loved her enough to give her the best life possible. We're glad that you will always be an integral part of her life.*
> *Thank you, Katelyn, for the best gift we've ever received. You've given us the love of our lives. We cherish her more than words can say.*
> *We're looking forward to seeing you again soon.*
> *All our love,*
> *Mallory and Buddy Carter*

I guess a lot of things in life are like that. You can't see the strength and character and enrichment you will gain until you've made it through the storm. Maybe that's what faith is all about. I noticed Katelyn prays every day now.

The members of our Avenues First Ward exceeded my expectations that Sunday at church. Many people went up to talk to Katelyn and to see how she was doing without the baby. Sister Dearborn found her way gently through the crowd and squeezed my arm so tightly it startled me.

"Well done, daughter of God," she said. Just like that. Her eyes were welling up with tears and she pursed her lips together. "I'm proud of you for being a true friend."

"It was nothing, really."

Sister Dearborn took both of my hands in hers. Her skin was soft and smooth. She looked straight into my eyes. "Yes, it was very much something, Avery. I don't think you realize the magnitude of what you've done."

"What do you mean?"

"You, Avery Rose, have saved two precious lives."

"You mean you knew about when Katelyn—"

"Yes, I knew. That's when I called you. She needed a friend, desperately. I was her leader and could only do so much. She needed someone on her level who could see her through this ordeal. Beyond a parent or church leader. She needed a friend. I knew that someone was you."

"Wow, I had no idea I was so key, or that the situation was that serious. All I could think about was how down she must have been feeling, how hard it is to feel left out and alone," I said, dropping my hands to my waist. "I've felt that way my whole life and I just wanted to ease her pain as best I could."

"That's the best thing any of us can do in this life, Avery."

We sat down in a nearby pew. I could hear the hum of the crowd around us and I could smell the mixture of perfumes and aftershaves. People were embracing Katelyn.

Still, I was focused on what Sister Dearborn was telling me. "When you think about it, that's all He really asks of us, that we look out for one another. And when we have a choice—try to do the right thing. If we mess up, there's always another choice around the corner. You chose the right thing by being such an amazing support to Katelyn without judging her. That's big."

"Well, when you say I saved two lives in the process, you'd better make that three. So many miracles have come my way this past year, in addition to Payton's birth. Ever since I returned from Italy, my life has changed. My dad and I made up and he's totally back in the picture now. My mom and I are getting along better. I even understand Grams better. She's an amazing lady."

Sister Dearborn chuckled.

I continued: "And, I'm not sure yet, but I think I might have found true love," I could feel the heat in my face from blushing. "I'm realizing it's been there all along—he has been there, but I just couldn't see it, before. I just feel really great overall, better than I can ever remember."

"It's called character," Sister Dearborn said. "You're growing into a remarkable young woman. You deserve every bit of happiness that's coming your way."

Sister Dearborn hugged me close. She smelled like honey, vanilla and hairspray.

"Sister Dearborn?"

"Yes?"

"Can I tell you something that you might think is really weird?"

"Go ahead. Tell me anything. What is it?"

"I had this strange connection with a woman in a painting while I was at an art gallery in *Florence*. I felt such a kinship with this woman I saw on canvas who lived several centuries ago. There was something in her eyes I could relate to. I've been writing to her in my journal ever since."

"Really?" Sister Dearborn's eyes widened and she crossed her arms.

"Do you think I'm nuts?" I asked, weakly.

"No, Avery, I don't."

"You don't?" I was surprised.

"Writing to her has really helped you work out a lot of things. That's what's important," said Sister Dearborn. "Besides, sometimes writing is the best way to deal with feelings that can feel so jumbled and complicated inside."

"But I've never even meet her, and will never meet her. And yet, I feel like I know her."

"Well," said Sister Dearborn. "You won't meet her in this life, but who knows about the next?" Then she winked at me and her eyes sparkled. "I think friendship is strong enough to last into the next life. Don't you?" Then she grabbed her Sunday book bag and put it over her shoulder. Sister Dearborn headed out of the chapel and down the hall. Then she was gone.

Dear Lucrezia,

Farewell, my trusted friend. This is the last time I'll write to you. Thank you for being the listener I needed.

I'm off to live my own life now. I know blessings are in store for me, more than I could've ever imagined, and in this century!

All my love,
Avery

13

The smell of cinnamon rolls baking in the industrial-sized ovens of the quaint restaurant downtown on Pierpont Avenue was intoxicating. The waiter brought a silver plate with two fat golden brown rolls and placed them in the middle of our table. Barclay folded his white cloth napkin in his lap and picked up the small glass bottle of maple syrup and drenched his cinnamon roll, letting loads of the sticky stuff seep into the plump folds and spill over the sides. He has always done this, as long as I have known him. He masks his breakfast in maple syrup. I've seen him put it on scrambled eggs and hash browns. Once, I remember watching him with amusement as he used syrup as a dipping sauce for his buttered toast.

I heard the clang of dishes behind the pewter double doors that led to the kitchen. Serving staff swung in and out at a frantic pace. Every table was full of people chattering with each other between succulent bites of eggs Benedict and French toast. Others took cell phone calls while trying to eat their blueberry whole-wheat waffles and spearing scrambled eggs with their forks.

"So, can you believe Katelyn actually did it? She signed the adoption papers and handed Payton over to the Carters," I broke off a crisp edge of my cinnamon roll and placed it in my mouth. I couldn't wait to get to the soft fluffy center, but I chewed slowly. I was nervous and wanted to be well mannered. "Mrs. Lundhausen was surprisingly unemotional when I called her with the news—all business. It's like, is that woman real? Or just a mannequin?"

"I'm sure she has to remain unattached to do her job." Barclay sopped up the syrup on his plate with a forkful of his sweet bread.

"How's Katelyn handling all of this?" he asked.

"She seemed gloomy this morning and yet, happy at the same time."

"I can understand that," Barclay said in between bites of cinnamon roll.

"You can?"

"Oh yeah, she's happy in her misery: story of my life."

"Are you miserable right now?"

"Sure I am, and I'm also having the time of my life. Is there ever anything else, any other way to be?"

"Of course there is, Barclay," I said around a mouthful of cinnamon roll.

"Not for me."

"Well I'm glad I make you so unhappy. We're off to a good start," I said, sarcasm mixed with the cinnamon on my tongue.

"You don't make me miserable, but the thought of losing you does. Every great thing in life has an equal but opposite reaction in its absence: rain and shine, light and darkness, love and loss." Barclay rested his fork on his plate and looked up at me. "And that's why we are here, right? So you can dump me like a hot potato?"

"No, no," I reassured while squirming in my seat. "Just to clear the air on a few things, you know, to talk." I picked up my crystal glass and took a swig of freshly squeezed orange juice.

Barclay waved his hand in the air and reached for more maple syrup. "I don't like the sound of this."

"Why, Barc? Why can't we talk about serious stuff?"

"We can. It's just I don't want the door hitting me in the

behind when we're finished." He doused his roll again.

"I just want you to know where I stand on something, before things get too complicated."

"They already are complex, Avie. Too late."

"Well, okay then. We have nothing to lose."

There was silence. We heard the low hum of dozens of conversations around us. They seemed to fade, as our conversation grew deeper and more sullen. I was scared I would offend Barclay by talking about the church, though this was precisely what I intended to do. It had always been a sore spot. I knew how painful it was to be the one always left behind.

"Barclay, first of all, I want you to know how much you mean to me."

"Uh-oh." He said with caution.

"What?"

"Here we go. I feel a 'but' coming on. You're a great guy, but…"

"No, really Barclay, what you did for me, making me my own personal prom night. That was amazing. How can I ever thank you? I couldn't have imagined a more magical, wonderful night. I'll remember it forever. And, my feelings for you are definitely growing stronger."

Even in the soft light of the restaurant I could see Barclay was turning a nice shade of red.

I took a deep breath and continued: "But the church is so important to me in my life. It's the one constant I've always had. It's my moral compass, I guess, that directs me when I'm confused and comforts me when I'm sad. I know the gospel is true."

Barclay nodded his head to let me know he was listening.

"I know it was hard for you growing up in Utah as a nonmember. I apologize for every member of the church who ever made you feel ostracized."

"That's a big G.R.E. word isn't it, Avie. Ostracized?" Barclay was mocking me and I didn't like his tone.

"I'm serious, Barclay. I'm trying to be sensitive here."

"What are you trying to say, Avery? Just say it already, will you? I can take it. I can take most anything." Barclay looked down at the black and white tile floor and let his mop of hair fall down over his forehead and cover his eyes.

"Well, I just want you to know where I stand on the issue of religion. I want to be true to you and to be honest with myself by making things clear."

"What things, Avery? I've known you just about my whole life. I'm fully aware that you're Mormon. It doesn't bother me."

"Bother you, why should it bother you?" I could feel the counterproductive sparks of anger rising through me.

"Whoa—what I mean is, I respect your beliefs. So what's the big deal?"

"Thank you," I said, trying to return to a calm, even tone. "That means a lot to me, Barc. You're such a great guy. I've never minded for a second that you aren't Mormon, you are such a good person."

"Hold on now, Avery. Aren't you being a tad judgmental? You don't mind that I'm not Mormon? Gee, thanks."

"I'm sorry, that's not what I mean. This isn't coming out the way I planned."

"Why do I feel like I'm on trial here?" Barclay straightened up in his seat across from me. "This, your attitude right now—feels terribly wrong; I don't recognize you like this Avery. It shouldn't matter what someone's institutionalized beliefs are. Think about it. How many wars have been fought in the name of religion? How many people have died because of it? And for what? To say they belong to some set of beliefs? That's a heavy price to pay. It's so hypocritical of religions that promote love and so-called brotherhood and turn around and fight, even kill. Heck, Avery, aren't you learning anything about being open-minded at the U?

Haven't you ever heard of a little thing called tolerance? Maybe you need to get out of Utah for a while."

I leaned forward and pushed my plate away. I was fuming and couldn't eat another bite.

"You've gone too far, Barclay. Who is judging whom now? We follow God's laws with faith. I don't claim to know everything. Besides, you wouldn't know anything about any organized religion anyway—especially mine. You don't even know what you believe." It's one of the downsides of knowing someone so well. When you fight you know exactly how to hurt.

"I know what I believe." Barclay's stare was cold and unwavering. "You've just never bothered to ask me."

"I'm listening," I folded my arms, expectantly.

"Put me on the spot, why don't you. I hardly think this is the time or place, Avery."

"Well?" I persisted.

"Well, I believe in God. I'm just not so sure that He always listens to me. I mean, look what happened to my mom. I prayed every night for her when I was little, just as you had taught me, and it didn't work. Why? Can you tell me why, Avery? Why would a loving God listen to some and ignore the pleadings of others?"

"I don't know," was my quiet response.

"Great, sounds like your religion is sure doing you a lot of good," he said, sardonically.

"Your mom was really sick, Barc. I don't know why and my heart aches for you, and for her. I do know that God cannot take away all the bad things that happen in life. But He grieves right along with us. And He can bless us in our time of need and help us through it. Suffering is a part of life and, unfortunately, it's the way we learn and grow. I don't know why, but I believe His knowledge is infinite. His timeline isn't linear like ours. He sees things from a different perspective."

"What does my mom killing herself have to do with

perspective? Where was God that day?"

I took a deep breath and fought the lump in my throat. "God is in the strength you've found to carry on, Barc. God is in the people who came to your doorstep that day and offered kindness, condolences and love. He was in little baby Kathryn's eyes when she looked at her mother for the first time in that tender moment in the delivery room. He was there again when he gave Katelyn the strength she needed to give her up. God works miracles, unexplainable, magnificent miracles. He also works through people—teaching them to serve one another and love one another. 'As I have loved you, love one another.'"

For a second there, I thought I saw tears welling up in his eyes. But then he seemed to compose himself using humor, typical Barclay defense mode.

"That's deep," he said with that grin of his I have always loved. My words had placated his anger and defensiveness. He took a hold of my hands. He was warm and strong.

He looked up at me, bashfully. "All I know is that love is love—no matter who you are or what you believe."

"I agree, Barc," I said nervously, my eyes darting down at the table and then back up at him again. "I just want you to know how important the church and the gospel are in my life. That's all. And it would be great if you'd come with me to Sacrament Meeting sometimes." I looked up at him, bracing myself. Had I gone too far?

"I'll go with you if you want, but no promises, Ave. I don't know if I can ever be one of them. You should know that."

"Fair enough. Just promise me this. Give it a real shot? Will you? Keep your mind open to the possibilities?"

"Hey, I think I can handle that. I threw you your own personal prom night, didn't I? I suppose I can 'investigate' your church. Isn't that what the missionaries call it?"

"Yeah, that's what they call it all right."

"Those missionaries knocked on my door so many times when I lived on I Street and I didn't let them in. Maybe the story's been passed down over the years. I'm a living legend with the Elders. I can see it now, I'll call them and they'll say, 'Whoa, that guy Barclay actually wants to talk to us? Miracles really do happen.' I'm sure that'll be right up there with the parting of the Red Sea." We chuckled.

Then he leaned in and kissed me.

I was exhausted when I returned home from talking with Barclay. Though painful, it felt good to assert myself, to let him know my deepest feelings. I flung open the door to my house to get inside and make a fire in the fireplace to thaw out. I was ready for spring to come. I longed to see bright pink and purple tulips pushing up through the snow. I loved the way the new Technicolor green grass always looked like it was dusted with powdered sugar after a late snow flurry. Kids would soon be foraging through the snow sprinkled grass for Easter eggs in their periwinkle fleece pants and gloves. Spring was right around the corner, but this night, it still felt like the dead of winter.

I pulled off my gloves, hat and coat and threw them on the floor near the sofa. I heard the clicks of Tigger's feet on the tile as she greeted me with happy panting. I reached down and scratched her bent ear and kissed her on her fuzzy head. In the light of the fire, I saw her wink.

I jumped when I discovered Katelyn was lying there sunken into the monster couch as still as an icicle. I found an old, brown fleece throw beside the couch and put it over Katelyn. She stirred in her sleep and snuggled up to the enormous pillows.

I tiptoed over to the fireplace and used one of the iron tools to coax it into a warm roar. As the fire began to crackle, it lit up the dark room in a brighter, warm amber glow. Katelyn looked peaceful and serene. I turned back around and that's when I noticed it: a package, neatly wrapped in brown paper with enough clear packaging tape to protect it from a nuclear attack. It was addressed to me. And in the top left-hand corner the return address read *Giuseppe Luchetti, Via delle Mazzini, 43, 84100, Firenze, Italia*.

"What could this be, Tigg?" I asked. She cocked her head to the side and stood at attention wagging her tail as if to say: "I don't know but I can't wait to find out!" I swear that dog of mine could understand English. When I spoke to her, those glossy black eyes told me she would love to respond, if only her snout could form those tricky words. How I loved that dog.

My heart began racing as my mind filled with memories of the handsome old painter with the raspy voice and flecks of silver in his black hair. I remembered how his deep-set wrinkles grew even more prominent when he spoke, showing years of living life to the fullest. He'd hold his paintbrush delicately in one hand and form sweeping gestures with the other as he spoke about the land he loved. Ah, Italy.

Why had he sent me a package? How had he tracked me down? I fiddled through Mom's junky drawers for some scissors to unleash the mystery. I found a rusty pair in the very back that appeared to have ceased operation in 1970 or so. I hoped it would do the trick for me anyway. Though the scissors were dull, they cut just enough that I could pull and tear through the stubborn packing tape and paper. It took some muscle, but I was running on adrenalin. The anticipation of what was inside was almost more than I could contain.

There, in the flickering glow of the fire, I saw a rectangular structure shrouded in packing foam and cardboard. I peeled back the layers around the corners, careful not to disturb whatever lay beneath. The fire was so hot on my face. It emitted a wonderful hickory scent as it popped and crackled, licking up the remainder of the kindling and turning into a roaring blaze. I stepped back away from the fireplace screen as I finished removing all the excess material.

It was a canvas, a rich painting in oils. I held it up to the amber light of the fire with all the delicacy of one holding a necklace of the most precious jewels. I will never, ever, forget what I saw next.

There, staring back at me from the canvas was a true beauty. Her crimson hair fell around her face and spilled onto her shoulders in thick ringlets. The delicate oils illuminated the glow of her pale skin, high forehead and supple chin. Faint pencil-thin arches framed her light green eyes. Her smallish lips were plump like a cherry with just a hint of shimmering gloss in the center. A crimson velvet wrap draped around her full white shoulders. She was radiant. What I appreciated most about her was the depth I saw in those intricately painted eyes. They seemed to leap off the canvas. Giuseppe captured the soul of this woman as he painted her gaze. Her essence was courageous, kind and full of infectious optimism. This was a woman who did not give up easily. She was always open to learning and discovering the route to becoming her best self, even if that path was full of potholes. The comely woman looking back at me reserved judgment of others, knowing there was always so much more to a person than her mistakes. The luminous lady sitting so regal in Giuseppe Luchetti's magnificent work of art was me.

14

An unruly lock of my hair wouldn't stay put. I tried to pin it back with the rest, which I'd pinned back away from my face in loose curls that cascaded down my back. The mirror was framed in ornate gold. It was peaceful and so quiet that I could hear the temple matron and another worker speak in whispers at the far end of the room. Both elderly women were dressed entirely in white. "She's a very attractive bride," the matron said, folding her slender arms at her thin waist and surveying me. The worker, shorter and plump around her middle, nodded in agreement. "Looks like they're going to be right on time, too," she said, tapping her watch.

My mother sat beside me wearing a crisp, light blue linen dress she bought for the wedding. She tilted her head to the side watching me while I powdered my nose and applied pale pink gloss to my lips. I wore a simple, white cotton dress, fitted through the bodice, with a full skirt that touched my ankles. My wedding gown, with the beaded bodice, scoop neck and princess waist, hung on a hook nearby for me to change into for pictures outside the temple after the ceremony. It looked regal, even just there on the hanger. Yet, somehow, the simple frock I wore for the temple was every bit as lovely.

Barclay had joined the church seven months after our heated discussion in the restaurant. He had started going to Sacrament

Meeting in Massachusetts, like he'd agreed. I'm sure at first he shifted in the pew and glanced frequently at the clock until the meeting was over. Then, during summer break when he was back in Utah and attending with me, he began staying for Sunday School and Priesthood Meeting, shrugging his shoulders and acquiescing. "Fine, I'll stay just this once," he had said.

Then, with a smile, he began talking with other ward members in between the meetings. He had avoided people at first. Afterward, we'd always cook a big meal of lasagna, thick slabs of cheese sandwiched between *al dente* pasta, served with buttered garlic bread, and share it with my mom.

Finally, one Sunday, he announced he was ready to get baptized. "I'm going on faith, Avery," he'd told me, before stepping in the clear water of the white tiled baptismal font. I had assured him that was good enough for me. We got engaged on a snowy night two years later. We planned the wedding for the week after he graduated from MIT in Aerospace Aeronautical, and I in English Literature with a minor in Art history.

Today, the big day had finally come. While my mom walked over and visited with the ladies in the bride's room, I took out my rumpled post card of *Lucrezia*. It was difficult to make out the small details of her face, like her eyelashes and her pupils, because the paper had worn so thin over time. Oddly enough, the distortion revealed something I'd never noticed before. Her expression, one I'd always taken to be haughtiness, I now recognized as something altogether different. *Lucrezia's* mouth was upturned in a slight smile that, combined with the look in her eyes and the curve of her arched eyebrows, emanated hope. Maybe that was what the skilled painter had seen in her and tried to capture many centuries ago. It wasn't that she was so much revered and sought after that made her attractive, as I'd thought before. *Lucrezia* was optimistic about her future.

In the celestial room, Barclay and I knelt across an altar and promised to love each other forever. Grams got misty-eyed and Papa put his arm around her to give her comfort. She straightened in her chair to regain composure, smoothing out her bright purple taffeta skirt that matched her pumps perfectly. My mom was crying silently, with dark lines of mascara streaming down her face. My dad was behind me with his hair slicked back to a high sheen. Janet loomed silently in a chair in the back, as if she was trying to remain as inconspicuous, invisible even, as possible.

Katelyn looked happier than I'd ever seen her. The dark circles were gone from beneath her eyes and the bags from fatigue had disappeared. And there was a luster to her skin that had been missing before. Even when she wasn't smiling, which was rare, her expression was content and her eyes showed joy. She sat in the front row holding hands with Brighton, her new boyfriend. He had strawberry blond hair cropped so short that it stuck straight up. He had a pronounced dimple on his chin and kind eyes. He was a returned missionary studying economics at the U.

Barclay looked more handsome to me that day than ever before. As I looked into his eyes, I couldn't believe we were there, in the temple together, getting married for time and all eternity. There was a time when he had said he would never set foot inside a church building. Now, he was one of us. And, he was about to become my husband. I was awestruck by the miracles that had happened in my life.

After having felt ostracized by Mormons for much of his life, he had practiced humility in seeking what he believed and then, he had the faith to follow it. Through Katelyn, I had learned what it meant to be a true friend and in the process learned to love myself. My mom and I had found peace. I'd accepted the fact that she would always annoy me a little, and I her, but that our love had no bounds. I now looked at Grams and Papa differently, too. No, their marriage wasn't perfect. But they had lasted through the tough times over the years and through it all, there was always love.

Barclay and I leaned in together and kissed tenderly across the altar.

*

A few weeks later, Barclay and I sank into the monster couch mom had passed down to us for a wedding gift, along with several shiny stacking shelves, bins and bookshelves. On the card that came with the gifts, she drew the word PACK RAT with a circle around it and a line drawn diagonally through it. "Start being organized early," she urged. "Don't make the same mistakes I did."

A dog-eared copy of *Sense and Sensibility* rested on my lap. "You'll never change will you," Barclay teased, eyeing the novel.

I shrugged my shoulders and he hugged me more tightly.

I snuggled into Barc. He smelled faintly of pine, Ivory soap with maple syrup on his breath. The fire crackled in the small fireplace in our tiny apartment, emitting a warm glow on our arms, hands and cheeks.

Earlier that day, we braved the cold to put flowers on his mom's grave.

Barclay was still exhausted from his long week at Thiokol. He is an apprentice on a team that builds rocket launchers for NASA. Once, falling in love had seemed as likely to me as traveling to the moon. Now, I'm married to a man who will help astronauts do just that.

The fire now was warm and comforting. The portrait of me hung above the simple mantle; the one Giuseppe Luchetti had painted for me. A small picture in a silver frame of four-and-a-half year old Kathryn Payton Carter sat beneath it. The Carters had sent us the picture of Kathryn smiling widely, revealing tiny white teeth. Her blond hair fell in wisps around her cherub-like face with a tiny nose and knitted brow. Katelyn still visited Kathryn each month faithfully and gave us regular reports on her many milestones; sitting up by herself, standing, walking and now drawing picture books about her great big family.

My eyes gazed back up to the painting and I studied it closely. As beautiful as the skilled brushstrokes were, with the delicate detail and gorgeous color palette, I couldn't help but pity the likeness of me in the portrait. Giuseppe had painted me at the beginning of that fateful trip with Grams and Papa. But I wasn't her anymore. I was no longer the tentative, discouraged woman full of self-doubt and insecurities. I now knew that true beauty came from within. This knowledge allowed me to share my life with Barclay, the boy who always knew me and had always loved me for who I was. Now, we would continue to grow together and cultivate the kindness and unconditional love in our own little family that drew us together in the first place.

I sighed and let my book drop gently to the floor at my feet. I put my legs over Barclay's, resting my head on the massive arm of the couch while he rubbed my bare feet. Then, I closed my eyes and drifted off into contented, blissful slumber.

ABOUT THE AUTHOR

© 2004 Kent Miles

Heather Simonsen is the author of three novels: the critically acclaimed *Sugar House Hill*, *Renaissance Beauty*, and *Horseshoe Bay*. She also wrote the authorized biography of the No. 1 pick in the 2005 NFL Draft, *Alex Smith: The story of the University of Utah's unlikely star quarterback*. She writes monthly feature cover stories for *The Salt Lake Tribune* on health & science and parenting issues. She has been featured in numerous publications, most notably *O, The Oprah Magazine*, *The New York Times*, and in *First for Women Magazine*.

She was a spokesperson for the 2002 Olympic Torch Relay. Heather was present when Muhammad Ali lit the cauldron in Atlanta. She was responsible for selecting 100 honorary 9-11 torchbearers and learned how resilient the human spirit can be. Heather was also a torchbearer and ran with the Olympic Flame in San Antonio, Texas, the city where she grew up. Heather was a celebrated television journalist for five years at ABC-4 television news in Salt Lake City before leaving the profession to raise her kids.

Heather earned high honors as a senior fellow and a magna cum laude graduate in journalism from the University of Texas at Austin. Heather earned a master of arts from Brigham Young University with a published thesis.

Heather has an identical twin sister, Holly Coyle, and three brothers. Her father, Stanley Wayment, earned his master's degree at Stanford University and his PhD from the University of Utah. He's a math professor at Texas State University. Her mother, Julia Wayment, is a homemaker and family history researcher. San Francisco 49ers quarterback Alex Smith is her first cousin.

She is the stay-at-home mother of two beautiful children: Halle Rose and Christian. Her husband, Soren, is an award-winning architect and city planner. The two restored their historic Salt Lake City home.

Heather loves gourmet cooking and baking. Her favorite cooking companions, though, are her kids. She also enjoys jogging in her neighborhood and hiking in the mountains. Heather is an avid reader. *To Kill a Mockingbird* is her favorite book.